DISEASES & DISORDERS

Childhood Obesity

M.N. Jimerson

LUCENT BOOKS
A part of Gale, Cengage Learning

GALE
CENGAGE Learning

Detroit • New York • San Francisco • New Haven, Conn • Waterville, Maine • London

LIBRARY OF CONGRESS CATALOGING-IN-PUBLICATION DATA

Jimerson, M.N.
  Childhood obesity / by M.N. Jimerson.
     p. cm. — (Diseases and disorders)
  Includes bibliographical references and index.
  ISBN 978-1-59018-997-9 (hardcover)
  1. Obesity in children—Juvenile literature. I. Title.
  RJ399.C6.J56 2009
  618.92'398—dc22

                                                           2008032328

Lucent Books
27500 Drake Rd.
Farmington Hills, MI 48331

ISBN-13: 978-1-59018-997-9
ISBN-10: 1-59018-997-3

Printed in the United States of America
1 2 3 4 5 6 7 12 11 10 09 08

Table of Contents

"The Most Difficult Puzzles Ever Devised"

Charles Best, one of the pioneers in the search for a cure for diabetes, once explained what it is about medical research that intrigued him so. "It's not just the gratification of knowing one is helping people," he confided, "although that probably is a more heroic and selfless motivation. Those feelings may enter in, but truly, what I find best is the feeling of going toe to toe with nature, of trying to solve the most difficult puzzles ever devised. The answers are there somewhere, those keys that will solve the puzzle and make the patient well. But how will those keys be found?"

Since the dawn of civilization, nothing has so puzzled people—and often frightened them, as well—as the onset of illness in a body or mind that had seemed healthy before. A seizure, the inability of a heart to pump, the sudden deterioration of muscle tone in a small child—being unable to reverse such conditions or even to understand why they occur was unspeakably frustrating to healers. Even before there were names for such conditions, even before they were understood at all, each was a reminder of how complex the human body was, and how vulnerable.

While our grappling with understanding diseases has been frustrating at times, it has also provided some of humankind's most heroic accomplishments. Alexander Fleming's accidental discovery in 1928 of a mold that could be turned into penicillin has resulted in the saving of untold millions of lives. The isolation of the enzyme insulin has reversed what was once a death sentence for anyone with diabetes. There have been great strides in combating conditions for which there is not yet a cure, too. Medicines can help AIDS patients live longer, diagnostic tools such as mammography and ultrasounds can help doctors find tumors while they are treatable, and laser surgery techniques have made the most intricate, minute operations routine.

This "toe-to-toe" competition with diseases and disorders is even more remarkable when seen in a historical continuum. An astonishing amount of progress has been made in a very short time. Just two hundred years ago, the existence of germs as a cause of some diseases was unknown. In fact, it was less than 150 years ago that a British surgeon named Joseph Lister had difficulty persuading his fellow doctors that washing their hands before delivering a baby might increase the chances of a healthy delivery (especially if they had just attended to a diseased patient)!

Each book in Lucent's Diseases and Disorders series explores a disease or disorder and the knowledge that has been accumulated (or discarded) by doctors through the years. Each book also examines the tools used for pinpointing a diagnosis, as well as the various means that are used to treat or cure a disease. Finally, new ideas are presented—techniques or medicines that may be on the horizon.

Frustration and disappointment are still part of medicine, for not every disease or condition can be cured or prevented. But the limitations of knowledge are being pushed outward constantly; the "most difficult puzzles ever devised" are finding challengers every day.

A Preventable Public Health Problem

The World Health Organization (WHO) states that "childhood obesity is one of the most serious public health challenges of the 21st century."[1] The incidence of childhood obesity has tripled during the past thirty years, and WHO estimates that as of 2007, at least 22 million children under age five and 155 million aged five to seventeen were affected worldwide.

In response to this alarming trend, WHO and other international and regional health agencies have initiated programs to prevent children from becoming overweight or obese. Although the terms *overweight* and *obese* are sometimes used interchangeably, health experts generally distinguish the two conditions by defining *overweight* as increased body weight relative to height based on standard height-weight tables, and *obese* as having an excessive amount of body fat compared to lean body mass. Research has shown that both conditions contribute to numerous health problems. Fortunately, says WHO,

overweight and obesity, as well as their related chronic diseases, are largely preventable. Governments, international partners, civil society and the private sector have vital roles to play in shaping healthy environments and making healthier diet options affordable and easily accessible. This is especially important for the most vulnerable in society—the poor and children—who have limited choices about the food they eat and the environments in which they live.[2]

Like the rest of the world, the United States has seen childhood obesity increase dramatically, with the U.S. surgeon general reporting that 17.1 percent (about 12.5 million total) of the children and adolescents in the nation aged two to nineteen are currently overweight, compared with 13 percent in 1999 and 5 percent in 1974. Since 2001, when U.S. Department of Health and Human Services secretary Tommy G. Thompson declared that "overweight and obesity are among the most pressing new health challenges we face today,"[3] the U.S. government has launched numerous initiatives to help prevent and reverse these conditions nationally in cooperation with parents, educators, and health-care professionals. In November 2007 the Office of the Surgeon General began one of the most comprehensive of these programs, called the Childhood Overweight and Obesity Prevention Initiative, Healthy Youth for a Healthy Future. This program encourages and helps communities throughout the country to promote healthy eating and increased physical activity among children and teens.

Challenges to Prevention Efforts

However, implementing preventive measures for childhood obesity is not a simple matter. Environment, behavior, and genetics all play roles in this epidemic, and most experts agree that obesity is a social problem as well as an individual medical issue. This means that many factors must be addressed when seeking prevention strategies.

Just a few of the environmental, behavioral, and social factors that researchers believe should be confronted are increased television and computer use; fewer physical activity programs in schools; suburban growth and urban crime that deter children from playing outdoors; and parents who offer high-salt, high-fat frozen meals or fast food to their children because they are too busy to prepare nutritious meals.

The resulting health problems, as well as the contributing causes of childhood obesity, have social as well as individual implications, since the diseases that are linked to obesity cost the government and the private sector billions of dollars each year and contribute to untold personal and family suffering. Children who are overweight are at greater risk for heart disease, type 2 diabetes, several types of cancer, bone and joint problems, asthma, and sleep apnea, all of which can lead to disability or early death. Such diseases account for seven out of ten deaths and affect the lives of 90 million Americans.

A school nurse in Pennsylvania weighs a kindergartener as part of a statewide effort to calculate and track students' body mass index. Schools and other groups in both the public and private sector are creating programs to combat obesity among children and teens.

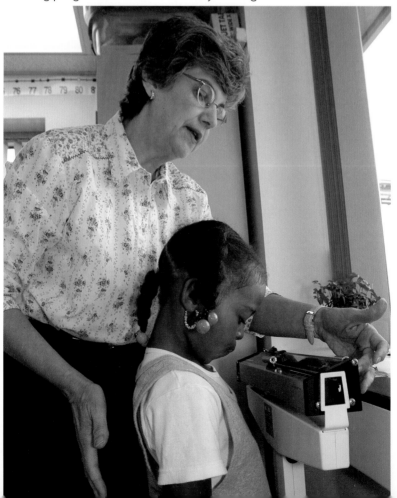

Chronic diseases are not the only hazards faced by obese children and teens. Social problems such as isolation, bullying, and discrimination, and psychological problems such as poor self-esteem and depression are also threats that may become chronic, since weight, once gained, is difficult to shed. In fact, losing excess weight can be so difficult that according to the Overweight Teen Web site, an obese six-year-old has a 50 percent chance of becoming an obese adult. If that child is still obese by ten years of age, the probability of becoming an obese adult rises to 70 percent. If one or both parents is also overweight, the obese child has an 80 percent likelihood of growing into an obese adult.

Why Prevention Is Preferable to Treatment

Health experts and government officials agree that, especially since it is so difficult for overweight people to lose weight, concentrating on obesity prevention efforts in childhood is a preferable first line of defense compared with relying on treatments in adulthood. Prevention provides an affordable and effective solution, especially since the costs of treating obesity-related diseases are extremely high. But since children have no control over the environments in which they live or the genes they inherit, solutions that emphasize individual self-control are less than effective. Advising children to be more active is pointless if children have no safe place where they can be active. Telling them to eat healthy food is also futile if access to unhealthy food is easy and access to nutritious food is not. Therefore, it is up to adults to create safer, more healthful environments so that any behavioral changes made by children can be effective in reducing their likelihood of becoming obese.

CHAPTER ONE

What Is Childhood Obesity?

Childhood obesity is a condition in which a child or teenager has excessive body fat. Some people view obesity as a weakness of character or a lack of willpower that allows an individual to eat so much that they gain tremendous amounts of weight, but experts are increasingly defining obesity as an actual disease. The American Obesity Association explains the reasons for this designation:

> Why do we think obesity is a disease? First, let's define our terms. Dictionaries agree: obesity is excess body fat. It is not defined as a behavior. Second, obesity fits all the definitions of "disease." Most dictionaries, general as well as medical, define a disease as an interruption, cessation or disorder of a bodily function, organ or system. Obesity certainly fits this definition.[4]

Too Much Fat

The disease known as obesity occurs when the body stores too much fat. Our bodies are composed of water, protein, minerals, and fat. All are needed for people to function. Lean body mass consists of the weight of muscles, bones, and internal organs made mostly of water, protein, and minerals. There are two types of body fat: essential fat and storage fat. Essential fat consists of necessary fat in the bone marrow, heart, lungs, spleen, kidneys, intestines, muscles, and nervous system. It is required as fuel for energy and for other body functions. Storage fat accumulates in adipose tissue, or fat cells, around internal organs and beneath the skin. Some storage fat is necessary for protection of organs and heat conservation, but too much results in obesity.

Doctors consider excess fat storage and obesity to be even more serious for children and teens than for adults, since obese children are at high risk for diseases such as type 2 diabetes and heart disease that traditionally affect only adults. Developing such diseases in childhood means that these children risk early debilitating complications and even early death. In addition, people who were obese as children have

Adipose tissue consists of round fat cells and connective tissue and makes up the layer of storage fat that is found underneath the skin and around internal organs. An excess of storage fat results in obesity.

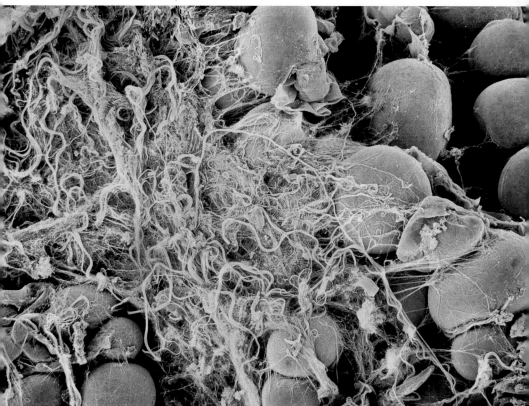

much more difficulty losing weight as adults because obese children develop an abnormally high number of adipocytes, or cells specialized for fat storage. These adipocytes remain with the person when they grow up; thus adults who were obese as children have more fat cells than normal. Adults who become obese during adulthood, in contrast, do not de-

Historical Views of Obesity

Throughout history people have held varying ideas about whether or not obesity is a disease and about whether or not it is desirable. Historians believe that the ancient Egyptians, for example, probably thought obesity was a disease because they placed statues of obese people alongside statues of people with other illnesses. In ancient Greece the renowned physician Hippocrates wrote about the fact that fat people were more prone to sudden death than were lean ones, and he recommended a combination of diet and exercise to help obese people lose weight.

In the mid-1770s in England, many people regarded obesity with interest and awe. Daniel Lambert, who weighed over 700 pounds (318kg), made a living by charging curious townspeople money to look at him. In the United States during the nineteenth century, most people believed that obese individuals were wealthy and secure. U.S. presidents Zachary Taylor, Millard Fillmore, Ulysses S. Grant, and Chester A. Arthur were all obese and were publicly regarded as prosperous, trustworthy, and upstanding—in large part because of their stature. During this era, fat cheeks, stomachs, and thighs made people appear "healthy" compared with the many who were emaciated by tuberculosis and other debilitating diseases prevalent at the time.

Today most people view obesity as unattractive and unhealthy, as prevailing standards of beauty equate thinness with attractiveness and as doctors reveal the link between obesity and serious illnesses.

velop new fat cells. Their existing fat cells simply grow larger. Since dieting and exercise can only shrink fat cells rather than eliminate them, those who are left with increased numbers of fat cells from childhood obesity have more difficulty losing weight.

Diagnosing Obesity

Defining how much excess fat constitutes obesity at different stages in life has historically varied among cultures. Doctors in many places traditionally determined whether or not an individual was obese by considering appearance or by referring to standardized tables that indicated an ideal body weight based on height, sex, and age. Since the obesity epidemic has spread throughout the world, however, WHO and various national health agencies have developed newer standardized criteria and measurements. Today, most experts measure body fat content compared to lean mass to assess whether someone is obese. They also look at where in the body the fat is distributed, because researchers have determined that people who store fat around the waist and abdomen are at much higher risk for cancer, type 2 diabetes, and heart disease than are those who primarily store fat in the hips and thighs.

Body Mass Index

The most common measurement used to diagnose obesity is the body mass index (BMI). This is calculated by dividing a person's weight in kilograms by their height in square meters. It can also be calculated by multiplying a person's weight in pounds by 703 and then dividing by their height in square inches. For example, the BMI for a sixteen-year-old girl who weighs 155 pounds and is 5 feet 4 inches tall is calculated as follows:

Step 1: 155 pounds x 703 = 108,965

Step 2: 5 feet 4 inches = 64 inches

Step 3: 64 inches x 64 inches = 4,096 inches

Step 4: 108,965 ÷ 4,096 inches = 26.6 BMI

Body mass index (BMI) can be used as an early warning sign that someone is at risk of becoming overweight or obese.

The BMI can be an indication that a person is underweight, of normal weight, overweight, or obese. A person with a BMI below 18.5 is considered underweight. A BMI between 18.5 and 24.9 means a person is of normal weight. A person with a BMI between 25.0 and 29.9 is regarded as overweight, and a BMI above 30.0 means a person is obese. Doctors further divide levels of obesity into three classes based on the health risks associated with increasing BMI. Class I, or mild obesity, consists of a BMI of 30.0 to 34.9 and places affected individuals at risk for health-related problems. Class II, or moderate obesity, is characterized by a BMI of 35.0 to 39.9 and involves a high risk of health problems. Class III, or morbid or extreme obesity, corresponds to a BMI greater than 40.0 and places the person at extreme risk. (The term *morbid* refers to life-threatening conditions.)

Although extremely overweight adults are routinely labeled obese, when it comes to children some experts worry about the shaming potential of the word *obese* and use the words *at risk of overweight* or *overweight* instead. The Centers for Disease Control and Prevention (CDC), for example, uses the word *overweight* rather than *obese* in defining the categories of childhood weight ranges. This can lead to confusion for parents and children alike, as pediatrician Vincent Iannelli explains:

The "At Risk of Overweight" category is especially confusing. Many people interpret that to mean that their child is at a healthy weight and "might" become overweight later. That category really corresponds to the adult overweight category though, and the child overweight category corresponds to the adult obese category. . . . While it certainly wouldn't be diplomatic to tell a child they are fat, to sidestep the issue and not get families the help they need is also wrong.[5]

Growth Charts

Since the bodies of children and teens are still developing, doctors also consider a child's age and sex when interpreting BMI. Infants, for example, generally have a higher proportion of fat to lean body mass compared to an active toddler, and fat distribution varies between teenaged girls and boys. For children ages two to twenty years, doctors calculate the BMI using the standard formula. They then plot the number on a BMI-for-age growth chart to see where an individual child ranks when compared with other children of the same age and sex.

In the case of the sixteen-year-old girl from the BMI calculation earlier, a BMI growth chart places her in the 90th percentile for her age, weight, height, and sex, because 89 percent of other sixteen-year-old girls have a lower BMI. According to the CDC guidelines, if a child's BMI is below the 5th percentile, the child is considered underweight. A BMI between the 5th and 85th percentile reflects a healthy weight. A child is viewed as at risk of overweight if his or her BMI is between the 85th and 95th percentile. A child whose BMI is above the 95th percentile is considered overweight. Therefore, based on a BMI-for-age growth chart, the sixteen-year-old girl who is in the 90th percentile is at risk for becoming overweight.

However, BMI and growth charts can only be used approximately to determine the proportion of fat to lean mass a person has. The sixteen-year-old girl may have a higher-than-average BMI, but if she is an athletic member of her school's tennis team,

Federal Agencies Fight Childhood Obesity

The U.S. Department of Health and Human Services (HHS) is the principal agency involved in developing standards for diagnosis; tracking statistics; and issuing research, treatment, and education guidelines for childhood obesity. HHS sponsors over three hundred programs administered by eleven operating divisions. Those divisions that are of particular relevance to childhood obesity are the National Institutes of Health (NIH), the Centers for Disease Control and Prevention (CDC), the Food and Drug Administration (FDA), and the Office of the Surgeon General.

The NIH conducts research of its own and funds the research of scientists in universities, medical schools, hospitals, and research institutions. It also helps train researchers and shares its findings with the public. Of the twenty-seven institutes that make up the NIH, those most closely involved with childhood obesity are the National Heart, Lung, and Blood Institute; the National Institute of Child Health and Human Development; and the National Institute of Diabetes and Digestive and Kidney Diseases.

The FDA assures the safety of food and drugs by approving, investigating, recalling, and banning certain products and issuing labeling standards. It provides public information on its activities and on public health topics.

The CDC monitors public health and develops preventive programs against disease. It provides information on health issues for people in every stage of life and is responsible for protecting Americans from health threats that exist throughout the world.

The Office of the Surgeon General is under the direction of the U.S. surgeon general, who is the primary federal health educator. The surgeon general and his or her staff oversee the operations of the U.S. Public Health Service and provide public information on ways to improve health.

the high BMI number of 26.6 might be due to muscle mass rather than excess body fat. Also, BMI cannot show where on the body fat is distributed, nor can it always reliably identify children at risk of becoming overweight. For example, a slim-boned child whose BMI is in the healthy range may actually be carrying excess fat. One study at the Children's Nutrition Research Center at Baylor College of Medicine in Houston, Texas, found that "one out of six children whose BMI value was in the normal range was found to have an unhealthy level of body fat. And one out of four with a BMI in the at-risk to obese range actually had a body-fat percentage in the normal range."[6]

Since BMI growth charts can sometimes lead to inaccurate diagnoses, doctors also use other techniques to calculate body fat. These techniques range from simple skin-fold measurements to assess how much fat is lying beneath the skin, to the use of precise technological equipment that calculates the amount of fat present in the body.

Skin Folds and Waist Circumference

In a skin-fold test, doctors measure the fat just beneath the skin—the subcutaneous fat layer—by carefully pinching a fold of skin between calipers. A caliper is a handheld tool that measures the thickness of fat in a given area of the body. There are many types of calipers. All have some sort of "pinchers" and levers, plus some type of engraved or electronic measurement markings. Skin-fold measurements of children are generally taken at the triceps, which is the back of the upper arm; at the calf, which is below the knee; and/or below the scapula, or shoulder blade.

Generally, girls between the ages of six and nineteen are considered overweight if their body fat is between 22 percent and 31 percent, and they are considered obese if their body fat is 32 percent or higher. A healthy range for girls is between 14 percent and 21 percent. Boys between these ages are considered overweight if their body fat is between 21 percent and 25 percent, and they are considered obese if their body fat is 25 percent or higher. A healthy range for boys is between 9 percent and 15 percent.

Another way doctors calculate body fat is to measure the child's waist circumference—the distance around the child's waist—using a fabric tape measure. Doctors have found that waist circumference is an effective and simple means of measuring central adiposity, or belly fat, in children. A large waist circumference indicates that fat is accumulating around the abdomen. The more fat that collects around a child's waist, the greater the risk that the child will develop diseases like diabetes, heart disease, high blood pressure, and some cancers. This is because abdominal fat is somewhat different from fat in the lower body, as explained by doctors at the Harvard University Medical School: "Fat accumulated in the lower body (the pear shape) is subcutaneous, while fat in the abdominal area (the apple shape) is largely visceral."[7] Visceral fat is more likely to increase the risk for certain diseases, because the type of fat cells that make up

A doctor uses calipers to conduct a skin-fold test on a young boy. A skin-fold test is one of several methods used to measure a person's percentage of body fat.

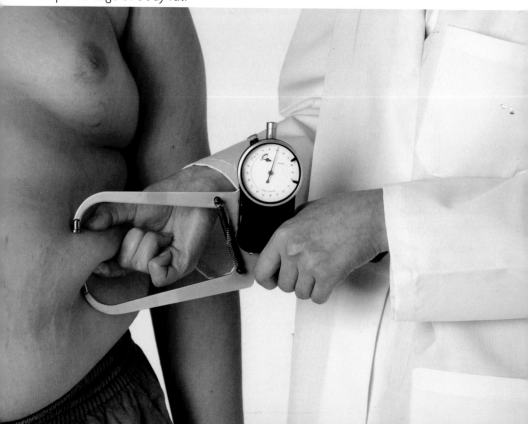

visceral fat release chemicals that disrupt the normal function of certain hormones such as leptin and adiponectin, which regulate appetite control and insulin effectiveness. Insulin is a hormone produced by the pancreas that enables the body to use carbohydrates for fuel. Visceral fat cells also release immune system chemicals called cytokines that lead to insulin resistance and chronic inflammation in the body, which may increase the risk of heart disease and other conditions.

Skin-fold tests and waist circumference measurements can easily be administered in a doctor's office, since they do not require specialized equipment. However, for more precise measurement of fat percentages and distribution, special machines are needed. These machines tend to be used mostly in research laboratories at medical centers because they are costly and require highly trained people to operate them. Doctors generally order these more sophisticated tests in cases where skin-fold and waist circumference measurements suggest that the child is at risk for overweight and the physician wishes to quantify precisely the distribution of bone, muscle, and fat so he or she can determine the severity of the risk and recommend appropriate lifestyle changes.

Measuring Fat Precisely

There are two types of machines for precisely measuring body fat: equipment that creates an image of where fat is stored and devices that determine lean body mass and use this information to calculate fat mass. Imaging techniques include CT, DEXA, lipometer, ultrasound, and MRI.

Computed tomography, or CT scan, combines X-rays and computer technology to create cross-sectional images of the organs, bones, muscles, and fat in the body. The images are more detailed than general X-rays and can reveal fat distribution, such as fat under the skin versus fat in the abdomen, which is an important indicator of disease risk. The main disadvantage of CT technology is that it exposes people to some radiation.

Like CT scans, dual-energy X-ray absorptiometry (DEXA) machines use X-rays, but doctors consider DEXA results more accurate than CT measurements in determining body composition. A DEXA machine sends two types of X-rays through the area being examined. The two types of X-rays have two distinct energy peaks, one of which is absorbed by soft tissue and the other by bone. This enables physicians to distinguish between bone, fat, and muscle mass.

In contrast to machines that utilize X-rays, a lipometer uses a light beam and a light detector. This small, portable optical device is held over an area of skin and relies on light reflected back from the skin to measure the thickness of subcutaneous fat. Although is it very safe and quick, a lipometer cannot measure visceral fat.

Like lipometers, ultrasound machines use reflected energy to measure body composition, but ultrasound uses high-frequency sound waves instead of light. A technician or doctor passes a handheld probe that resembles a microphone over the skin of the body area being analyzed. Sound waves penetrate the skin and bounce off fat, bones, and muscles and return to the ultrasound machine, which records the length of time elapsed. This data is converted by a computer into measurements of the thickness, shape, and composition of each body part through which the sound waves passed, and doctors can use these measurements to determine body fat content in different areas. Different ultrasound machines have varying levels of power and imaging quality. Some give two-dimensional pictures of the internal body parts, while others offer three- or four-dimensional images. All are very safe and quick procedures. However, it is difficult to obtain accurate estimates of total body fat with this method.

The fifth type of imaging technology is magnetic resonance imaging (MRI). MRI machines use a magnetic field and radio wave pulses of energy to generate two- or three-dimensional images of the body's internal organs. The images are so precise that they can be used to determine tissue composition, making them useful in measuring where fat cells are distributed on certain organs.

There are some disadvantages to MRI machines. Since the patient must lie in a long, narrow cylindrical tube that is me-

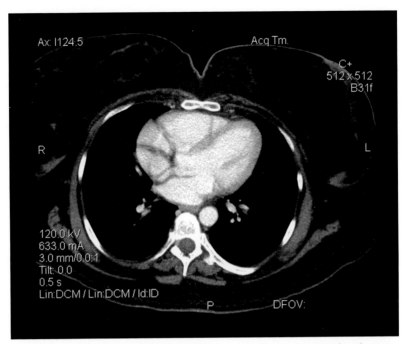

An image from a CT scan of an obese person's torso reveals a large layer of fat surrounding the chest cavity. CT scans are one of several high-tech methods of obtaining a precise measurement of body fat.

chanically drawn into a very small, narrow chamber, people who are very large may not fit in an MRI scanner. MRI machines are also loud and require that the person remain absolutely still, sometimes for more than twenty minutes, so they may not be a practical option for very young children, who may feel trapped and frightened.

Nonimaging Techniques

Nonimaging techniques used to precisely measure body fat include air displacement plethysmography, hydrostatic weighing, and bioelectric impedance analysis. Air displacement plethysmography, also known as BodPod, relies on the physics of Boyle's law, which states that as pressure goes up, volume goes down, and vice versa. First a technician weighs the child using a standard scale. Then the technician measures the volume of air in each of the two chambers that make up the egg-shaped BodPod, which is large enough to accommodate a person who weighs up to 550 pounds (249.5kg). The child then sits in the first chamber, known as the test chamber, and the door is closed. The second, smaller chamber, called the reference chamber, remains empty. Computerized pressure sensors determine the amount of air displaced by the child's body in the first chamber and compare it with the amount of air in the

An obese man's body fat percentage is determined via bioelectric impedance analysis, which uses electrodes that send electrical currents through the body. The amount of resistance to the current indicates a measurement of body fat.

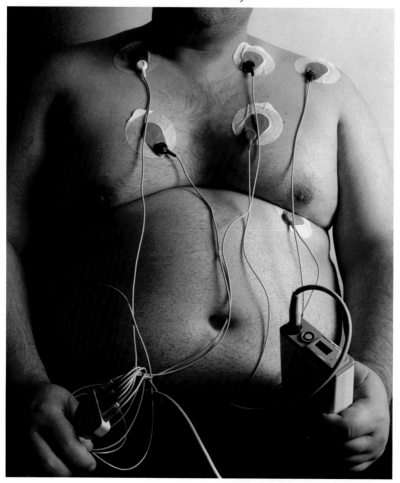

second chamber. The reduced amount of air volume in the first chamber is equal to the volume of the child's body. The child's weight is then divided by the body volume to establish the body's density, which is the concentration of matter contained in the body. Fat tissue has a higher density than lean tissue, and the computer can calculate the fat and fat-free densities after analyzing the child's height, weight, age, and volume. Experts consider the BodPod to be a very accurate method of determining lean and fat body mass.

Hydrostatic weighing (hydrodensitometry, or underwater weighing) is similar to air displacement plethysmography in accuracy but measures the displacement of water instead of air. It relies on the physics of Archimedes' principle, which states that the buoyant force on a submerged object is equal to the weight of the fluid that is displaced by the object. First a technician weighs the child on dry land. Then the child sits in an underwater plastic chair that is connected to a scale, blows all the air out of his or her lungs, and places his or her head underwater for five to ten seconds while the scale measures the underwater body weight. The body volume is determined by subtracting the body's weight on land from its weight underwater and dividing this number by the density of the water. The body volume is then used to calculate the body density and the percentages of lean and fat body mass. Since the subject needs to be completely submerged underwater, this form of measurement is not suitable for very young children.

Bioelectric impedance analysis is used to measure the resistance within the body to a flow of electric current passing through it. Lean tissue offers little resistance, but fatty tissue has high resistance, making it possible to determine the percentage of fat present. The procedure is quick and simple, but various factors, such as body temperature, time of day, and how hydrated the body is, can influence the accuracy of the results.

Once a child has been diagnosed with obesity, health-care providers can move on to the next phase: treatment. Treatment is essential, because left untreated, obese children are at risk for a range of serious health conditions.

CHAPTER TWO

Increased Health Risks of Childhood Obesity

Obese children are at risk of developing a variety of psychological and medical disorders, and experts agree that both sorts of problems can be dangerous to their well-being. Among the serious health conditions they may face are metabolic syndrome, cardiovascular disease, high cholesterol, high blood pressure, diabetes, and cancer.

Metabolic Syndrome

According to the American Heart Association, approximately 1 million adolescents aged twelve to nineteen have metabolic syndrome, which is a term used to group together several medical conditions that often occur concurrently. Three quarters of these adolescents are overweight, and around one in four is at risk of overweight. These figures indicate that overweight is a significant risk factor for the syndrome. In addition, the National Health and Nutrition Examination Survey, 1988–1994, found that the higher the weight, the greater the risk.

The conditions that make up metabolic syndrome are obesity, high blood pressure, hyperinsulinemia (high insulin levels), and dyslipidemia (high levels of triglycerides and bad cholesterol and low levels of good cholesterol). Having just one of these conditions significantly increases the risk of diabetes and heart disease, and if more than one of these conditions are present, the risk is even greater. This is why doctors emphasize that early detection and treatment of the syndrome are important.

Cardiovascular Disease

Whether or not they have metabolic syndrome, obese children are at high risk for cardiovascular disease, the leading cause of death in the United States. *Cardiovascular disease* is a blanket term that covers several disorders of the heart and

An illustration shows the development of atherosclerosis, as fatty plaque builds up along the walls of blood vessels in the heart, limiting or blocking the flow of blood. Atherosclerosis is a leading cause of coronary artery disease, one of several conditions that obese children are at risk of developing.

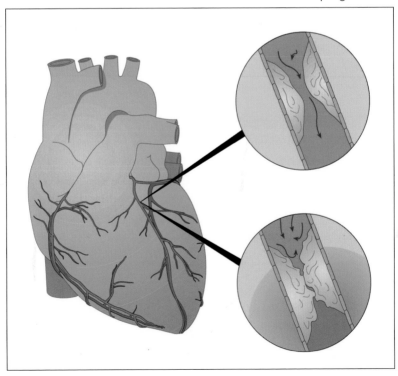

blood vessels that seriously impair the heart's ability to function properly. These disorders include coronary artery disease, atherosclerosis, and hypertension.

Coronary artery disease, also known as coronary heart disease, is a narrowing of the small blood vessels that supply blood and oxygen to the heart. Coronary artery disease is usually caused by a condition called atherosclerosis.

Atherosclerosis occurs when plaque made up of fatty substances, cholesterol, cellular waste products, calcium, and other substances sticks to the inside walls of the arteries. As the coronary arteries become narrowed due to the buildup of arterial plaque, blood flow to the heart slows down or even stops, causing chest pain (angina) and heart attack.

A heart attack is also called a myocardial infarction, coronary thrombosis, or coronary occlusion. Heart attacks result when the blood supply to part of the heart muscle (the myocardium) is severely reduced or stopped when arterial plaque tears or ruptures, creating an obstacle where a blood clot forms and blocks the artery. If the blood supply is cut off for more than a few minutes, muscle cells suffer permanent injury and die from lack of oxygen, which can disable or kill the victim, depending on how much heart muscle is damaged.

High Cholesterol

A high level of cholesterol in the blood (also called hypercholesterolemia) is a major risk factor for coronary artery disease and heart attack. Cholesterol is a soft, fatlike substance found in the bloodstream and cells. It is mainly produced in the liver, but it also enters the body when a person eats animal-based foods, such as egg yolks, meat, fish, and poultry. Cholesterol is essential to the body and is used to form cell membranes and some hormones.

Since cholesterol and other fats cannot dissolve in the blood, they have to be transported in the bloodstream by two types of carriers called lipoproteins: low-density lipoprotein (LDL) and high-density lipoprotein (HDL). Lipoproteins are a combination of protein and lipids. Lipids are fatty acids, such

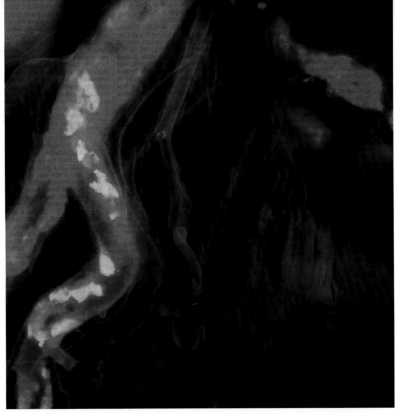

An image of the human heart shows a buildup of cholesterol, highlighted in yellow, inside an artery, resulting in a blockage. Excessive levels of LDL cholesterol in the bloodstream are associated with both heart attack and stroke.

as cholesterol and triglycerides. Lipids are created by the liver and delivered by the bloodstream to the cells that need them in order to function.

LDL has been labeled "bad cholesterol," because excess amounts in the bloodstream can slowly build up in the inner walls of the arteries. HDL is known as "good cholesterol" because high levels of HDL seem to protect against heart attack, while low levels of HDL increase the risk of heart disease. Medical experts think HDL helps carry LDL cholesterol away from the arteries and back to the liver, where it is removed from the body.

Like cholesterol, triglycerides are made in the liver and can enter the body when a person eats animal-based foods. Triglycerides are chains of high-energy fatty acids that form the main energy stores for the body. Hormones regulate the release of triglycerides from fatty tissue, making energy available for the body to use. Physical inactivity and a diet very high in carbohydrates can result in high triglyceride levels. Many people with obesity, high blood pressure, and/or diabetes also have high triglyceride levels.

People with high triglycerides often have a high total cholesterol level, including a high LDL level and a low HDL level. Excess levels of fats such as triglycerides or LDL cholesterol in the blood are known as hyperlipidemia, a condition associated with increased risk of heart disease and stroke. A stroke occurs when blood flow to the brain is suddenly interrupted by a blood clot or plaque blockage, or when blood vessels in the brain rupture, an event called a hemorrhagic stroke. This in turn causes the death of brain cells in the affected areas, leading to disruptions in the part of the body controlled by that part of the brain. Paralysis; mood and behavior changes; and loss of vision, speech, or memory can all result from stroke.

A nine-year-old girl participating in a research project on childhood obesity has her blood pressure checked. As obesity rates rise, children are increasingly susceptible to developing high blood pressure.

High Blood Pressure

Also known as hypertension, high blood pressure is called a "silent killer" because people are often unaware that they have it. "Kids with high blood pressure often don't have any symptoms, so the condition can be tough to catch,"[8] says an article on the KidsHealth Web site.

High blood pressure occurs when blood is pumped through the vessels with excessive force. It can cause blood vessels to rupture and lead to heart disease or stroke, and it is increasingly appearing in young people. "Once considered only a threat to adults, high blood pressure is now affecting more children— jeopardizing their potential for a healthy future,"[9] says the Mayo Clinic. Experts say it is also one of the most preventable forms of cardiovascular disease; losing excess weight, consuming less salt, and increasing physical activity are all important preventive measures.

Diabetes

Diabetes is another danger facing children who are obese. Diabetes is a chronic disease in which the body does not make or properly use insulin, a hormone needed to convert sugar and other food into energy. Children with diabetes have increased blood sugar levels due to an absence of insulin, or due to their body's failure to respond to insulin's effects. High concentrations of sugar build up in the blood and spill into the urine to be excreted from the body. As a result the body loses its main source of fuel. There are three types of diabetes that affect children: type 1, type 2, and hybrid diabetes. Type 1 is not usually associated with obesity, though type 2 is. Some overweight children have a combination of type 1 and type 2, known as hybrid diabetes.

Type 1 Diabetes

Type 1 diabetes is also known as insulin-dependent or juvenile diabetes. It is a chronic autoimmune disease in which the immune system destroys the insulin-producing beta cells of the pancreas. It can occur at any age, but most often begins in children and adolescents. Since the pancreas can no longer

Measuring Blood Pressure

A person's blood pressure is measured in millimeters of mercury (mm Hg) by an instrument called a sphygmomanometer. A nurse or doctor wraps the sphygmomanometer cuff around the individual's upper arm and inflates the cuff with an inflation bulb until blood flow in the brachial artery stops. The examiner then listens to the sounds in the artery with a stethoscope while slowly releasing the pressure in the cuff. When blood flow begins, the examiner hears a whooshing or pounding sound as the heart contracts and pumps blood. The pressure viewed on the measuring unit attached to the cuff when the sound starts is the systolic blood pressure. When the pressure is further released and the sound can no longer be heard as the heart is at rest, the pressure at this point is recorded as the diastolic blood pressure. The systolic pressure number over the diastolic pressure number is the blood pressure reading, such as 125/80. Whether or not a child's blood pressure is considered healthy depends on the child's sex, age, and height. According to the tables issued by the National Heart, Lung, and Blood Institute, a child may have high blood pressure if the measurement is higher than the 95th percentile for other boys or girls of the same age and height.

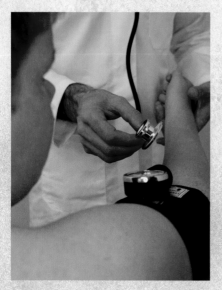

A young boy gets his blood pressure checked by a doctor using an instrument called a sphygmomanometer.

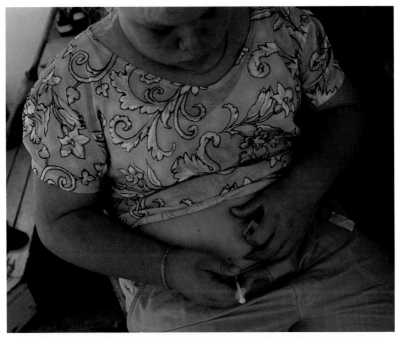

A twelve-year-old girl with diabetes injects herself with insulin in order to regulate her blood sugar levels. Children who are obese are at increased risk of developing the disease.

produce insulin, people with type 1 diabetes require daily injections of insulin for life.

Symptoms of type 1 diabetes usually develop over a short period of time and include increased thirst and urination, constant hunger, weight loss, and blurred vision. Children also may feel very tired. If not diagnosed and treated with insulin, a child with type 1 diabetes can lapse into a life-threatening diabetic coma, known as diabetic ketoacidosis.

Type 2 Diabetes

Type 2 diabetes is also known as insulin-resistant diabetes. In the first stages, the body becomes resistant to insulin, requiring increasing amounts to control blood sugar. Initially the pancreas responds by producing more insulin, but after several years, insulin production may decrease, and diabetes develops. Type 2 diabetes used to occur mainly in adults who were overweight and over forty years old. Now, however, with more children and adolescents becoming overweight, type 2 diabetes is occurring more often in young people. Some studies suggest that the percentage of children diagnosed with type 2 has increased from less than 5 percent before 1994 to 30 percent to 50 percent in recent years.

Symptoms of type 2 diabetes are tiredness, thirst, nausea, and frequent urination, and they usually develop slowly in children. For Jennifer, who was diagnosed with type 2 diabetes at age fourteen, the primary symptom was fatigue. "I just thought I was tired because I was heavy,"[10] she said. Other symptoms may include weight loss, blurred vision, frequent infections, and slow-healing wounds or sores. Some children or adolescents with type 2 diabetes may show no symptoms at all. Physical signs of insulin resistance include acanthosis nigricans, a condition in which skin around the neck or in the armpits appears dark and thick and feels velvety.

Hybrid Diabetes

Overweight children may have elements of both type 1 and type 2 diabetes. This condition is known as hybrid, or mixed diabetes. Children who have it are likely to have both the insulin resistance associated with obesity and type 2 diabetes, and the beta cell antibodies associated with autoimmunity and type 1 diabetes. Symptoms are the same as for type 1 and type 2 diabetes.

Complications of Diabetes

Excess sugar in the blood can lead to serious complications in all types of diabetes. One common complication is blood vessel damage, which can affect numerous parts of the body. For example, neuropathy, or nerve damage, results from injury to the walls of the tiny blood vessels that nourish the nerves, especially in the legs. This damage can spread, leading to eventual loss of feeling in the legs.

The kidneys can also be affected when the millions of tiny blood vessels that filter waste from the body are injured. This condition is called nephropathy. The earlier diabetes develops,

Diagnosing Diabetes

A doctor diagnoses diabetes by ordering urine and blood tests. A urine test reveals whether or not the patient is excreting excess glucose or ketones (acids that build up in the blood when the body burns fat for energy because it cannot use carbohydrates due to insulin deficiency). Blood tests measure exactly how elevated glucose or ketone levels are. One type of blood test is a fasting plasma glucose test. This measures blood sugar after the patient has fasted for at least eight hours. A fasting glucose level greater than 126 milligrams per deciliter (mg/dl) indicates that the person has diabetes. Another blood test is an oral glucose tolerance test. This measures blood glucose levels two hours after the person has consumed a sugary beverage. If the level is at 200 mg/dl or higher, the person is diagnosed with diabetes. A blood ketone level of 0.6 millimoles per liter (mmol/L) or greater indicates that the individual is in danger of diabetic coma.

the greater the threat it poses to kidney health. Severe damage can lead to kidney failure or end-stage kidney disease, which cannot be reversed and requires dialysis (cleaning of the blood using a special machine) or kidney transplant.

When the blood vessels of the retina at the back of the eye are damaged by diabetes, it is a condition called diabetic retinopathy. Diabetes can also lead to cataracts (clouding of the lens of the eye), glaucoma (elevated pressure in the eye), and eventually blindness.

Poor blood flow to the feet, along with nerve damage in the feet, can result in various foot complications. Untreated cuts and blisters on the feet can become so seriously infected that affected limbs must be amputated. Bacterial and fungal skin infections, as well as itching, are common with diabetes.

Diabetes treatment can sometimes cause blood sugar levels to drop too low, a condition known as hypoglycemia. Taking

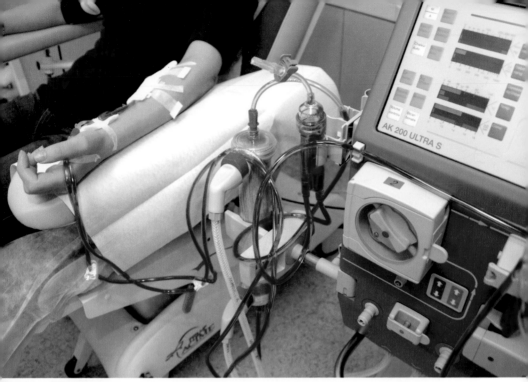

A patient is hooked up to a dialysis machine that filters toxins from the bloodstream. Kidneys damaged by diabetes or other disorders can lose their ability to clean the blood, making dialysis necessary.

too much insulin, missing a meal, or exercising too much may cause hypoglycemia. A child can become irritable, shaky, and confused. When blood sugar levels fall very low, loss of consciousness or seizures may occur.

Hyperglycemia is a condition where blood sugar levels are too high. It can be caused by eating too much, getting too little exercise, having an illness, or forgetting to take medications on time. Over time, hyperglycemia can damage the eyes, kidneys, nerves, blood vessels, gums, and teeth. In addition to these complications, "data shows that a child under age 14 who develops Types 2 diabetes loses as much as 27 years from his or her life span,"[11] says William Klish of Texas Children's Hospital.

Cancer

In addition to cardiovascular disease and diabetes, cancer poses a threat to the health of obese children. Many forms of cancer, including cancer of the breast, ovaries, prostate, kidney, colon, and pancreas, have been linked to obesity. High fat levels can interfere with the body's normal production of hormones, which are the chemical messengers that regulate activity in various parts of the body. Disruptions in hormone activity can lead to cancer cell development.

Cancer is a general term for diseases characterized by uncontrolled, abnormal growth of cells. The resulting mass, or tumor, can invade and destroy surrounding normal tissues. Cancer cells from the tumor can spread through the blood or lymph (the clear fluid that bathes body cells) to start new cancers in other parts of the body and can be fatal if left untreated.

Long-Term Consequences of Childhood Obesity

As more and more conditions that used to be considered adult diseases are affecting obese children, health-care professionals have become concerned that serious complications such as amputations, vision loss, and dialysis could become a common occurrence among young people, and life expectancy could actually decrease. "Obesity has been shown to have a substantial

This chart lists the many risks associated with childhood obesity.

Risks associated with childhood obesity

- ✓ Cardiovascular disease
- ✓ Degenerative joint disease
- ✓ Depression
- ✓ Early puberty and early start of menstruation in girls
- ✓ Eating disorders
- ✓ Exposure to social prejudice and discrimination
- ✓ Fat accumulation in the liver (fatty liver/liver disease)
- ✓ Gallbladder disease
- ✓ High cholesterol
- ✓ Hypertension
- ✓ Increased anxiety and stress
- ✓ Joint pain
- ✓ Low self-esteem
- ✓ Sleep apnea
- ✓ Type 2 diabetes mellitus

negative effect on longevity, reducing the length of life of people who are severely obese by an estimated 5 to 20 years. . . . Unless effective population-level interventions to reduce obesity are developed, the steady rise in life expectancy observed in the modern era may soon come to an end and the youth of today may, on average, live less healthy and possibly even shorter lives than their parents,"[12] states an article in the *New England Journal of Medicine*. In response to this threat, governments, communities, and individuals are implementing programs to prevent this worst-case scenario from ever becoming grim reality.

CHAPTER THREE

What Causes Childhood Obesity?

According to an article in the medical journal the *Lancet*, the body systems that control weight are so finely tuned that if a child's energy consumption exceeds energy expenditure by only 120 calories a day—the energy in one serving of sugar-sweetened soda—then over a ten-year period that child could gain up to 110 pounds (50kg) of excess weight. A calorie is a unit of heat that measures the amount of energy a particular food gives the consumer. The energy gap—the difference between energy needed and energy actually consumed—lies at the heart of the current childhood obesity epidemic.

Four major factors influence the energy intake/expenditure equation: diet, physical activity, environment, and genes. These factors generally occur in combination; for example, poor nutrition coinciding with lack of exercise. Diet and exercise have the most impact on weight, says the U.S. Department of Health and Human Services: "Poor diet and physical inactivity, resulting in an energy imbalance (more calories consumed than expended) are the most important factors contributing to the increase in overweight and obesity in this country."[13] The environment in which children live, in turn, affects what they eat and how often they exercise. Inherited genes and problems with hormone-producing body systems can also play a role in weight gain.

Poor Diet and Nutrition

Poor diet and nutrition can negatively affect mood, self-esteem, and school performance as well as weight and the risk for diabetes and other health problems. According to the U.S. Department of Health and Human Services dietary guidelines, a healthy, nutritious diet needs to include daily servings of foods that provide important nutrients. The number of daily servings recommended varies with the person's size and caloric needs, but generally includes four to six servings of whole grains; four or five servings of fruits and vegetables; two or three servings of low or nonfat dairy products; one or two servings of lean meat, poultry, or fish; three or four servings of nuts and legumes; and plenty of water. In addition, the Department of Health and Human Services recommends that people consume certain amounts of vitamins and minerals such as calcium each day.

However, the Department of Health and Human Services reports that 80 percent of high school students do not eat adequate

High school students line up for fried, high-fat foods in a cafeteria. The tendency of children and teens to consume unhealthy, high-calorie foods over fruits, vegetables, lean proteins, and whole grains is a major contributor to the rise of obesity.

amounts of fruits and vegetables. Only 39 percent of children aged two to seventeen meet the U.S. Department of Agriculture's dietary recommendation for fiber, which is found primarily in dried beans and peas, fruits, vegetables, and whole grains.

Not only are children not eating enough healthy foods, but they are also consuming energy-dense, unhealthy foods. Energy density is the amount of energy contained in a specific amount of food. It is measured in kilocalories per gram or kilocalories per milliliter, which is the energy released when the food is eaten and absorbed. Fats contain the highest energy densities, about 9 kilocalories per gram. Carbohydrates (sugars) and proteins are around 4 kilocalories per gram. Instead of the fresh fruits and vegetables, whole grains, fish, lean meat, milk, and water recommended by *Dietary Guidelines for Americans, 2005,* children are living on highly processed, high-fat, high-sodium fast foods and sugar-laden candy, baked goods, and soft drinks. Processed foods generally contain few nutrients and many calories.

Children are also skipping breakfast and compensating by consuming more at lunch and dinner. Studies have shown that "eating small frequent healthy meals (instead of two or three large ones) has been associated with being thinner and having a better cholesterol profile."[14] Indeed, some physicians recommend that obese children spread out their caloric intake over several small meals rather than two or three large ones to help with weight reduction and to cut down on the sharp rises in blood sugar that accompany consumption of large amounts of food.

Super-Sized Portions

In addition to concerns about the quality of food that children are consuming, health experts are also worried about the quantity. During the 1980s, portion sizes of packaged and convenience foods began increasing regularly, as food sellers sought to win business from their competitors. By offering larger portions, food sellers promoted the idea that more food for the same amount of money was a better deal. And customers, interested in getting the most for their money, began to assess the value of food by portion size instead of by nutritional benefit.

A first grader compares two potatoes as part of a lesson on portion sizes and nutrition. In order to indicate value, the amount of food provided at restaurants and in prepackaged foods has increased since the 1980s, causing people to eat more than they may realize, a factor some experts link to rising obesity levels.

Several studies have shown that when people are given a larger portion in a restaurant or in prepackaged foods, they do not realize they are eating more. As the CDC explains: "For example, bagels or muffins are often sold in sizes that constitute at least 2 servings, but consumers often eat the whole thing, thinking that they have eaten 1 serving. They do not realize that they have selected a large portion size that was more than 1 serving."[15]

Some researchers have done studies that indicate that the increase in portion sizes has contributed to the childhood obesity epidemic. For instance, one study at the Pennsylvania State University Departments of Nutrition and Human Development and Family Studies found that "body weight was positively related to energy intake and portion size . . . children regulate energy intake largely through portion size."[16]

Super Size Me

Filmmaker Morgan Spurlock heard about two teens who sued McDonald's, claiming the fast-food chain made them obese. He decided to find out for himself what effect eating nothing but food from McDonald's would have on his body and recorded his experience in his documentary film *Super Size Me.*

For thirty days, Spurlock ate at McDonald's three times a day, tried everything on the chain's menu at least once, and always accepted the super-sized food portion option if it was offered. At the beginning of the month, the thirty-two-year-old director was examined by three doctors and found to be in good health. However, because he was consuming a diet high in sugar, sodium, and fat, his health worsened rapidly. In an interview with *DVD Times,* Spurlock explained, "Over the course of the movie I was eating probably an average of between 4500 and 4900 calories a day, and out of all those calories I was getting less than half of the vitamins and minerals that my body needs . . . from twice the amount of calories." He put on 25 pounds (11.3kg), his cholesterol levels and blood pressure

shot up, he experienced chest pains, his liver function declined, and he became tired and depressed. Afterward, it took him fourteen months to lose the weight he had gained.

Quoted in Matt Day, "Exclusive Interview with Morgan Spurlock, Director of *Super Size Me,*" *DVD Times.* www.dvdtimes.co.uk/content.php?contentid=55390.

Filmmaker Morgan Spurlock tracked the effects of his month-long experiment of eating nothing but food from McDonald's in his 2004 documentary *Super Size Me.*

However, other experts writing in the *American Journal of Clinical Nutrition* have pointed out that no one has proved that the increase in portion sizes has actually caused the increase in obesity: "Increases in portion size have occurred in parallel with the rise in the prevalence of obesity, which suggests that large portion sizes could play a role in the increase in body weight."[17] However, the researchers caution that the studies do not show that increased portion sizes directly cause obesity. These researchers also emphasize that the energy density, or number of calories, in a particular food, rather than just the size of the portion, has a significant effect on whether or not the food contributes to weight gain.

Limited Physical Activity

In addition to poor nutrition and oversized food portions, children's activity levels also have a bearing on childhood obesity. However, instead of getting adequate exercise, children today are leading increasingly sedentary lives. Less than a quarter of children walk or bike to school, compared with more than two-thirds a generation ago. A 2002 survey discussed in the journal the *Future of Children* found that the main reason 66 percent of parents gave for their children not walking to school was that school was too far away. Too much traffic, fear of abduction, crime in the neighborhood, and children not wanting to walk were also given as reasons. One percent even cited a school policy against children walking to school as the reason.

The CDC notes in a 2007 study that reductions in school requirements for physical education classes have also led to less physical activity among children and teenagers. The number of schools requiring physical education (PE) dropped significantly in grades one through twelve compared with numbers in the early 1990s. For those students who do participate in PE classes today, the study showed that only a third of adolescents were actually physically active for more than twenty minutes, three to five days a week.

Recess, another opportunity for children to be physically active, is also being edged out of the school day. The National

Grade school students run and play during recess. Children often have limited opportunities to be active during the day, as walking to and from school has given way to driving or bussing in many communities, and cuts in physical education classes and recess time for budget reasons have affected many schools.

Association for Sport and Physical Education recommends that schools provide supervised, daily recess for students up to grades five or six. However, in 2000 a School Health Policies and Programs Study found that 29 percent of elementary schools provide no recess for kindergarteners through fifth graders.

Environmental Factors

The environment, or surroundings, in which children live can significantly affect the amount of physical activity they participate in. It can also expose them to nonnutritious, energy-dense foods instead of healthy dietary alternatives. Since children have limited skills when it comes to making healthy choices, if they are placed in unhealthy environments the likelihood is that they will become unhealthy. The main environments in

Requirements for Physical Education in Schools

Health experts are concerned that the fact that many schools do not require adequate amounts of physical education has contributed to the childhood obesity epidemic. In many states, high school students are only required to participate in PE classes for one of their four years of high school. Some schools allow students who are involved in extracurricular sports to be excused from PE. Currently, only one in three high school students take daily PE classes. In middle schools, PE requirements range from 55 minutes per week to 275 minutes per week. In elementary schools, some localities mandate as little as 50 minutes per week, while others require up to 200 minutes per week. The National Association for Sport and Physical Education, the CDC, the American Heart Association, the National Association of State Boards of Education, and the American Academy of Pediatrics recommend at least 150 minutes per week for elementary school students and 225 minutes for middle and high school students.

which children live and grow include the built environment, school, the home, and society.

Unhealthy Environments

The built environment is the physical, human-made setting in which people live their lives. The built environment has changed significantly over the past forty years. Many people now live in cities, where children may have little or no access to playgrounds, parks, basketball courts, or baseball fields. Grocery stores with affordable fresh fruit and vegetables may be located many miles away from the home. Lack of sidewalks and bike paths combined with increased automobile traffic may make walking and cycling hazardous. Fast-food restaurants with large portion sizes of cheap, animal-based, unhealthy foods and sugary beverages are everywhere. The result is that there are few opportunities for children to be physically active and to eat nutritious foods.

Snacks and Soft Drinks in Schools

Most children spend the majority of their waking hours in school. With tightened budgets, schools have sometimes chosen to sacrifice physical education offerings and recess in favor of spending their limited money on academic offerings, which are viewed as more essential to a child's future success. To make money for their operating or expansion costs, some school districts have entered into financial arrangements with soft-drink and snack-food manufacturers to allow the companies to set up vending machines on school campuses. Usually the school districts receive financial compensation, such as a

High school students walk past a soft drink vending machine in the hallway of their school. Many school districts receive money from snack or beverage companies in exchange for making their products available for sale on school grounds.

percentage of the income from sales, donations from the snack or beverage manufacturers toward needed school equipment or scholarships, or donation of beverages or snacks to fund-raisers for the schools.

In 2004 the American Academy of Pediatrics issued a policy statement regarding the damaging impact on child health when soft drinks and snack foods are consumed in school. They found that 40 percent of children's daily energy intake was supplied by added fats and sugars, with sugar-laden drinks the primary source of the added sugar. Each 12-ounce (355ml) sugary soft drink consumed daily is associated with a 0.18-point increase in a child's body mass index (BMI) and a 60 percent increase in risk for obesity.

Targeted Advertising

After school, children typically engage in sedentary activities, turning to television, the Internet, and video games for entertainment. Not only is watching television a sedentary activity, but the advertising children see also promotes poor eating habits.

Children of all ages are exposed to a huge amount of advertising for unhealthy food and beverages. Children who are eight to twelve years old are especially at risk because they watch the most television and see the most food ads, yet do not receive adequate education in nutrition or fitness. They are also likely to spend less time with their parents, to have their own money, and to have many opportunities to make their own food choices. With its stream of soft-drink, fast-food, cereal, and snack-food advertisements targeted toward children, television is a considerable risk factor for childhood obesity.

Less Family Time

Today many children grow up in homes with only one parent, or in homes where both parents work. With limited time available, parents may rely on snacks and convenience foods that are quick to prepare but are high in fat, sugar, and salt and low in nutritive value. Parents may not have the time or energy to

Today, due to many reasons, children watch more television and engage in too little physical activity.

supervise or participate in outdoor play or activities, thus modeling unhealthy behaviors for their children.

Children living in low-income communities are at greater risk for obesity than those living in wealthier communities. Their parents are more likely to have to work longer hours to meet living expenses and are unable to afford a babysitter or other supervision for their children while they are at work. The home neighborhood is more likely to be unsafe, offering few recreational areas where children can be physically active. Consequently, children living in less-affluent areas end up staying indoors by themselves after school, watching more television than children who have the luxury of safe outdoor areas to play.

The Prenatal/Perinatal Environment

Parents may also have an impact before birth and just afterward on a child's risk for becoming obese. Some researchers suspect that prebirth overnutrition or undernutrition on the part of the mother may trigger childhood and lifelong obesity. They speculate that if the mother is obese, the transfer of excess nutrients through the placenta to the unborn child may stimulate a permanent change in appetite, nerve, and gland functioning, or the rate at which energy is used up. Maternal obesity seems to correspond with high birth weight of the child and obesity later on in the child's life, although it is unclear whether this link is due to genes inherited from the mother or to excess nutrition in the womb. Possibly excess nutrition is the significant factor, since a 1998 study comparing two female rats with the same gene type—one obese due to overeating and the other of moderate weight—found that the offspring of the obese rat were heavier.

Prebirth undernutrition may also affect the unborn child, predisposing it to gaining and retaining weight. Maternal undernutrition would teach the unborn child's developing brain to expect limited food availability after birth, and one way of doing so would be to program the developing brain to be less sensitive to leptin—a hormone produced by fat cells that tells the body when it has eaten enough, reducing appetite and speeding up metabolism. Children who are resistant to leptin and given access to plenty of food at some point after birth would continue to eat past the normal point of satiety—the psychological feeling of being full and satisfied—even if they had already accumulated large supplies of stored energy in the form of body fat and its accompanying large supplies of appetite-reducing leptin.

Just after birth appears to be another key time when a child's risk for obesity can be established. Bottle-feeding instead of breast-feeding, for example, may raise a child's risk for obesity. One explanation could be that breast-fed babies tend to control the length of a feed, turning away from the breast when full. Parents of a bottle-fed child might encourage the child to finish the bottle, disregarding the infant's subtle cues that it has eaten enough and training the child to do likewise—a habit that can last a lifetime.

Heredity

According to an article in the *Future of Children,* as much as 25 percent to 40 percent of BMI may be inherited. Evidence supporting a relationship between heredity and weight gain is supplied by results from long-term studies of identical twins, some of whom were raised together and some of whom were raised apart. Since identical twins share the same DNA, the studies can provide useful information about whether certain diseases are inherited or whether they are caused by external influences such as diet.

One study in 1990 at the University of Pennsylvania School of Medicine found that identical twins raised apart are very likely to have gained similar amounts of weight over time despite growing up in differing environments. What is also interesting is that this correlation was almost as close (0.7) as the match in

Long-term studies of identical twins have provided evidence supporting a relationship between heredity and weight gain. However, childhood obesity has risen too rapidly to be explained by genetic variants alone.

weight gain between identical twins raised together in the same household. (A correlation of 1.0 is a perfect match.) This suggests that environment is not necessarily the major determinant in the development of childhood obesity; instead, genetics may play an even greater role than expected.

Another 1990 study titled "The Response to Long-Term Overfeeding in Identical Twins" demonstrated that some people are genetically more likely to gain weight than others. It found that within each pair of twins fed a fattening diet, their weight gain matched; each twin in the pair put on a similar amount of weight. However, when weight gain in one pair of twins was compared with weight gain of twins in another pair, the amount of gain differed, indicating that gene variance or mutation may play some role in a child's predisposition or tendency to become obese.

Genes may play a role in childhood obesity, but the rate at which this epidemic has risen over the past three decades is too rapid to be explained by genetic variants, since such changes take many thousands of years to spread throughout a population. Poor diet, physical inactivity, and an altered environment—all of which have changed significantly over the past thirty years—remain the prime suspects in the childhood obesity epidemic.

CHAPTER FOUR

Treatment

Once a child or teen becomes obese, media and societal pressures to lose weight may motivate that individual to resort to dangerous methods in an attempt to shed pounds and inches quickly. According to the CDC, "A nationwide survey [in 2005] found that during the 30 days preceding the survey 12.3% of [high school] students went without eating for 24 hours or more; 4.5% had vomited or taken laxatives; and 6.3% had taken diet pills, powders, or liquids without a doctor's advice."[18]

Such extreme attempts to control weight drain essential minerals (electrolytes) from the body. Kidney damage, abnormal heartbeat, muscle weakness, seizures, and heart attack are some of the serious problems caused by abrupt mineral loss. Even if young people are informed of these dangers, they may lack the good judgment needed to believe and avoid them, so they require guidance and support from health-care professionals and family members.

Following a weight-loss program can interfere with a child's growth and development, so it is rarely the primary treatment for childhood obesity. Instead, the aim is to slow or stop weight gain so a child can grow into his or her appropriate weight. However, a gradual weight-loss program may be recommended for extremely obese children with a BMI for age and sex greater than the 95th percentile.

Treatment Options

A team of health-care professionals that includes doctors, nurses, dieticians, and exercise specialists designs a treatment plan tailored to each child's needs. They consider how overweight the child is; any health complications; psychological issues such as depression; the child's age, sex, and activity level; whether the child has somewhere safe to play and exercise, and whether the child has access to nutritious foods. Treatment methods may include behavior modification, drug treatment, or more extreme options, like dental wiring, surgery, or alternative living environments. Whichever methods are chosen, an article in the journal *Pediatrics* stresses that "treatment programs should institute permanent changes, not short-term diets or exercise programs aimed at rapid weight loss. Methodic, gradual, long-term changes will be more successful than multiple frequent changes."[19]

Behavior Modification

Behavior modification treatment, which aims to change behaviors such as eating unhealthy foods and not exercising, is appropriate when an obese child does not have serious medical complications. Several factors affect the outcome of behavior modification. First, treatment should begin as early as possible; the older the child, the more likely his or her obesity will persist into adulthood. Second, both child and family need to be willing to change. If the family is unwilling, family counseling may be recommended to explore why.

When the child and the family are ready to change, education is their most valuable tool. Health-care providers can train family members to be more aware of what they eat and how active they are and show them how to track and improve both. An appropriate behavior modification strategy encourages gradual, manageable changes in diet and activity and keeps motivation high through praise rather than criticism.

Improving the Diet

Dietary improvements emphasize nutritious meals and a healthy approach to eating. Since the risk of diabetes, cardiovascular disease, and some cancers increases dramatically with weight, support organizations for these diseases advocate diet guidelines that are similar to those put forth by the U.S. Department of Health and Human Services and the American Dietetic Association.

One factor that these organizations say is important in improving the diet of family members is ensuring that families eat meals together to improve closeness and communication, model healthy eating behavior, and strengthen the family support system. As Sheah Rarback of the American Dietetic Association notes, "Research has found strong links especially between the food mothers eat and the choices made by their children. And children's eating

A boy selects an apple for a snack. Behavior modification treatment teaches children to be mindful of the foods they are choosing and to make healthy food choices.

Carbohydrates

Refined and processed carbohydrates	Whole-grain and high-fiber carbohydrates
White bread	100% whole-wheat bread
White rice	Oatmeal
White potatoes	Brown rice
Pasta	Whole-wheat pasta
Sugary cereals	Whole-grain crackers
Cinnamon toast	Popcorn
Sweets	Cornmeal
Jellies	Hulled barley
Candy	Whole-wheat bulgur
Soft drinks	Bran cereals
Sugars	Rye wafer crackers
Fruit drinks (fruitades and	English muffins
fruit punch)	Dry beans and peas
Cakes, cookies, and pies	Navy beans
Dairy desserts	Kidney beans
Ice cream	Split peas
Sweetened yogurt	Lentils
Sweetened milk	White beans
	Pinto beans
	Green peas
	Soybeans
	Whole fruits, fresh, frozen,
	or canned
	Vegetables
	Low-fat milk

This table displays the different foods containing refined and processed carbohydrates and whole-grain and high-fiber carbohydrates. Dietary guidelines provide information on the healthiest foods to eat and which foods to avoid, as well as how much to eat.

behaviors are influenced by such family-related factors as the number of meals eaten together."[20] Family involvement from an early age is therefore key in helping a child develop and maintain healthy eating habits. Families are advised not to eat out often, since it is easier to control the content, quality, and preparation methods of meals made at home.

Dietary guidelines and education by health professionals inform families about the healthiest foods to eat, how much to eat, and which foods to avoid. The National Institutes of Health stress that fat intake should be unrestricted before two years of age because fat is essential to healthy brain and body development during that time. After age two, foods high in saturated fats and cholesterol, such as fatty meats and some vegetable oils, and foods high in sugar are best limited because of their damaging impact on weight and cardiovascular health.

Increasing Physical Activity

Dietary changes alone cannot help a child reach or maintain a healthy weight. Physical activity is an essential part of an effective

Shaq's Big Challenge

In June and July 2007 a six-part reality television show hosted by Shaquille O'Neal aired on the ABC television network. In the show, which was called *Shaq's Big Challenge*, the then Miami Heat basketball star along with a team of specialists including a physician, personal trainer, nutritionist, celebrity chef, and coach worked for nine months with six obese children aged eleven to fourteen to help them lose weight and get healthy. Together they met with the six middle schoolers in their homes and schools in Broward County, Florida, to help them improve their eating and exercise habits. The goal of the show was to confront the childhood obesity epidemic by demonstrating how a fitness plan centered on nutritious, inexpensive meals and increased physical activity could provide a model for similar programs in communities across Florida and the United States. The children in the show had starting weights ranging from 182 to 285 pounds (82.5 to 129.3kg) and lost weight in amounts ranging from 25 to 77 pounds (11.3 to 35kg) as a result of Shaq's challenge.

weight management program. The American Heart Association recommends that parents limit children's sedentary activities to allow them more time for physical activity. "Limit television time to at most 2 hours per day,"[21] they advise in an article in the journal *Circulation.*

The U.S. surgeon general recommends sixty minutes per day of moderate to vigorous physical activity at least five days per week for children and adolescents. For example, walking briskly is moderate activity, while jogging or running is vigorous activity. Children unable to manage this level of activity because of their weight or health condition need an exercise plan tailored to their fitness level. Children unaccustomed to exercise also do better with encouragement, praise, sensitivity, and patience from their support system. They are most likely to stick with physical activities that are easy to integrate into

A boy rides a bike in a park. It is important for children to be physically active as part of their daily routine. Some communities are promoting bike riding as part of a healthy lifestyle. As a result, safe and accessible bike paths and bike lanes are being implemented to encourage more bike riding.

their daily routine, such as walking or biking to school or going outside to play. They will also stick with physical activities that they find fun or interesting.

For adolescents, an effective activity program should combine resistance training with aerobic activity. In resistance training, the muscles work against an opposing force to develop strength, such as in lifting weights. Aerobic activity, on the other hand, improves heart and lung fitness and stamina. Walking, jogging, running, swimming, and dancing provide good aerobic workouts.

Family Involvement

Obese children need family support if they are to enjoy the benefits of exercise and improved diet. A recent nutrition and physical activity survey by the American Dietetic Association Foundation showed that parents are strong role models for their child's behavior, including their eating habits—more so than anyone else. The survey found that "regardless of age, children report that a parent is the person he or she 'would like to be like most.'"[22] Parents who eat healthy foods and participate in fitness activities with their children have the opportunity to forge a supportive, communicative relationship and model a healthy lifestyle.

Parents may wish to be good role models, but some may be concerned about triggering an eating disorder in their overweight child or damaging their self-esteem. Some parents may therefore be reluctant to bring up the issue of overweight. Others may hope their child will grow into their weight without outside intervention. Some do not even realize their child is overweight, interpreting the extra pounds as a sign that their child is receiving adequate nutrition. Still others assume their child is healthy if they do not currently have serious medical problems with highly visible symptoms. The mother of Malri, an obese five-year-old in Tanzania, Africa, for example, resists health-care workers' efforts to encourage her to provide healthier foods for her son because she believes "rounded forms run in the family—we have no history of chronic diseases, so why make a big fuss of all this?"[23]

A mother prepares a healthy meal with her daughter's help. A family network of support, including parents who serve as positive role models, is important for helping obese children improve their health.

When parents are unwilling to play a role in reducing a child's obesity, the child may need to leave the home, perhaps moving to a foster home and obtaining treatment from there, or attending a weight-loss summer camp or residential pediatric obesity program that offers behavior modification therapy, physical activities, nutrition education, and peer support. Wherever these lifestyle changes are promoted, sometimes they are not enough to offset life-threatening complications of obesity. In such circumstances, radical treatment methods may be considered.

Radical Treatment Methods

According to an article in the journal *Future of Children*, "Experts suggest that children and adolescents with a BMI greater than the 95th percentile for age and sex and with obesity-related medical complications that may be corrected or improved through weight reduction should be considered for intensive regimens."[24] These intensive, or radical, treatment methods, which may include calorie restriction, dental wiring, and gastric (stomach) surgery, differ from treatments that center around simple changes in diet and exercise in that they require careful supervision and monitoring by a doctor to minimize the chances of malnutrition, side effects from medications used, and complications from surgery.

Calorie Restriction

Calorie-restricting diets may be administered at a pediatric obesity center that specializes in research and treatment. Food intake is reduced to 600 to 900 kilocalories per gram per day, and carbohydrates and fats are strictly limited. At least 51 ounces (1.5L, or six glasses) of water are also consumed with this protein-based diet to help the kidneys flush the toxic by-products of protein breakdown from the body. Lean meat, poultry, fish, beans, soy, nuts, whole grains, and low-fat milk are all protein sources. The diet is supplemented with vitamins and minerals. Weight regain can be a problem when the diet is over, so a lifelong commitment to healthy eating and exercise is very important.

Dental Wiring

Calorie restriction can also be achieved by wiring the jaw shut. Brackets are attached to upper and lower teeth, and the jaws are wired together to block out solid food. A gap left between the teeth allows the patient to consume a balanced diet of liquefied food through a straw. Children with dental problems, allergies, breathing difficulties, or binge-eating disorders should not undergo this procedure. Although the diet includes the carbohydrates, protein, fat, vitamins, and minerals necessary to maintain good health, the treatment is easily sabotaged with high-calorie liquids like milkshakes, sodas, and sports drinks. As doctors from the Duke University Weight Loss Surgery Center explain, poor success rates make this treatment uncommon today: "Large clinical studies demonstrated a median weight loss of 55 pounds but after four months the weight loss reached a plateau.

When the wires were removed, patients regained 100 percent of the lost weight. Many patients failed to lose significant weight as they learned to sip high calorie fluids through straws."[25]

Bariatric Surgery

Bariatric, or weight-loss, surgery is more extreme than dental wiring. It is a last resort when calorie restriction has failed for extremely obese adolescents with life-threatening complications of obesity-related diseases. The surgery is a last resort because of concern over children's limited ability to understand the consequences of the life-changing surgery and the lack of information available about long-term consequences. Although it is still performed infrequently in adolescents, teen bariatric surgery in the United States increased from just over two hundred procedures in 2000 to almost eight hundred procedures in 2003.

Most doctors will not perform bariatric surgery on anyone under age fifteen. Those under eighteen whom they will treat this way must have attained physical maturity, have been unsuccessful in losing weight after six months of doctor-supervised calorie restriction, have a BMI of at least 40, and have serious obesity-related diseases. Sixteen-year-old Brittany, for example, weighed over 400 pounds; had high blood pressure, insulin resistance, and sleep apnea; and tried numerous diet and exercise programs before doctors approved her for surgery.

Adjustable Gastric Banding

There are two major types of bariatric surgery: adjustable gastric banding (AGB) and Roux-en-Y gastric bypass (RYGB). For those patients who qualify for bariatric surgery, the choice of methods depends on the individual's needs and condition. AGB is simpler and offers a faster recovery time, but results in slower weight loss than RYGB. However, the slower weight loss of AGB may be safer for adolescents, since their bodies are still developing, and the procedure is reversible.

In AGB the doctor places a silicon band around the stomach to mold it into an hourglass shape. The egg-size upper portion of the stomach fills quickly when food is eaten and stays full longer

Who Is a Candidate for Weight-Loss Surgery?

The Surgical Weight Loss Program for Teens at Cincinnati Children's Hospital Medical Center identifies several factors that make a teen eligible for obesity surgery. The teen must have been unsuccessful with other organized weight-loss attempts. A body mass index of 40 or more combined with obesity-related health problems are additional requirements. Doctors therefore look for such obesity-related health problems as type 2 diabetes and obstructive sleep apnea. Other health problems they look for include high blood pressure and high levels of cholesterol and triglycerides. Asthma, joint and back pain, depression and anxiety, and being unable to participate in daily activities are additional factors doctors consider.

Health problems are not the only criteria for eligibility. Eligible candidates must be able and willing to follow nutrition guidelines before and after surgery. They must demonstrate that they understand the risks and benefits of surgery, as well as the fact that they are making a life-long commitment to a healthy lifestyle and medical monitoring. Informed, highly motivated teens with considerable family support and realistic expectations of the surgery are more likely to succeed, so psychologists interview the family to assess the level of commitment and family support.

A teen who recently underwent obesity surgery at the Cincinnati Children's Hospital Medical Center sits with his mother, also a surgery patient. Doctors consider many factors before approving a teen for obesity surgery.

since food passes slowly into the larger lower portion of the stomach through the channel created by the band. Although forced to eat smaller amounts of food at a time, the patient feels satisfied.

The band is inserted through a small keyhole incision with the aid of a tiny camera, so the procedure is quick, lasting roughly one hour, and requires a hospital stay of about a day. The band can be tightened or loosened by surgery as the patient needs. On average patients lose a pound a week, but weight regain is a risk unless the patient eats right and exercises. Complications may include slippage of the stomach up through the band or blockage when solid food gets trapped in the channel, both of which require surgery to resolve.

Roux-en-Y Gastric Bypass

RYGB results in more weight loss than AGB at first, although after three years, the final weight loss is about the same. Doctors recommend RYGB for people who must lose large amounts of weight fairly quickly for health reasons. The surgery is more complicated than AGB and is also irreversible because it involves permanently restructuring the stomach and small intestine. RYGB reduces the quantity of food patients can eat and also limits the absorption of nutrients and calories by bypassing part of the small intestine.

The stomach is separated into two pouches using surgical staples or a band. The small intestine is also separated into two parts so that the duodenum (the upper part of the small intestine) and a few inches of the jejunum (the lower part of the small intestine) remain attached to the lower, larger stomach pouch. The top of the lower jejunum is attached to the upper, smaller stomach pouch through an incision to form the Roux limb, or food channel. The bottom of the upper jejunum is rejoined to the small intestine at a point lower down the jejunum to form the bileopancreatic limb, which carries acids from the stomach and digestive juices from the liver, pancreas, and small intestine to meet the food traveling through the roux limb. The result is a Y shape consisting of roux limb, bileopancreatic limb, and lower small intestine.

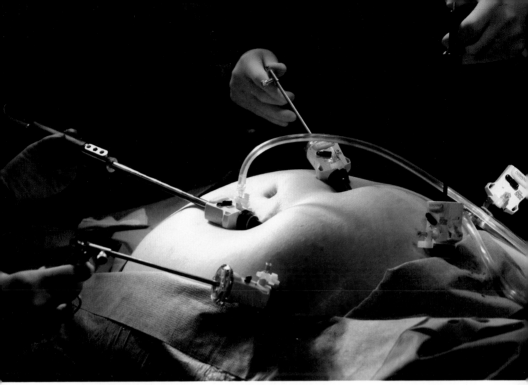

An obese patient undergoes Roux-en-Y gastric bypass surgery, in which the stomach is divided and the digestive tract rerouted, decreasing the capacity for food in the stomach and limiting the amount of calories absorbed by the body.

Since food bypasses the upper small intestine, there is less opportunity for nutrients and calories to be absorbed, and the result is rapid weight loss. This can lead to a shortage of nutrients, however, which can be particularly severe in the first days after surgery when the patient may also vomit as the body adjusts. Lifelong mineral, vitamin, and protein dietary supplements are therefore essential following RYGB.

Possible complications from RYGB include internal bleeding, blood clots, and anastamotic leakage, which is seepage through the surgical staples between the stomach and intestine. This potentially serious occurrence can lead to infection requiring antibiotics or even another surgery. Thick scar tissue may also develop, creating blockages that also require surgery to fix. Dumping syndrome can be a problem too, caused by sugar being dumped into the intestines. Normally, the stomach slowly releases food through the pyloric valve into the small intestine. Following RYGB, however, undigested food bypasses

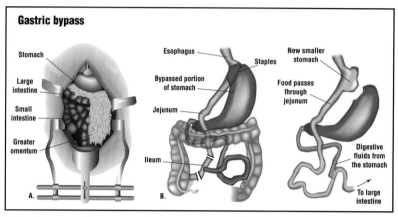

Gastric bypass

This diagram shows a Roux-en-Y gastric bypass. A large incision is made down the middle of the abdomen (A). The stomach is then separated into two parts, as is the small intestine. The top of the lower jejunum is attached to the upper, smaller stomach pouch through an incision to form the Roux limb, or food channel. The bottom of the upper jejunum is rejoined to the small intestine at a point lower down the jejunum to form the bileopancreatic limb. The result is a Y shape consisting of roux limb, bileopancreatic limb, and lower small intestine.

the lower stomach and enters the small intestine rapidly, triggering the body to pull water from the bloodstream to dilute it. Symptoms, which last thirty to forty minutes, include dizziness, rapid heartbeat, cold sweats, anxiety, cramps, and diarrhea. The syndrome is not life-threatening, and patients quickly learn to avoid it by not consuming fatty and sugary foods.

RYGB requires lifelong changes in eating habits. The new stomach pouch only holds about 2 or 3 ounces (59 to 89 ml) of food, so small portions of carefully chewed soft or pureed foods are eaten, allowing a few minutes between each swallow. Liquids are drunk between meals—not during—to avoid dumping syndrome, vomiting, and feeling full before enough nutrients have been eaten.

Drug Treatments

Because bariatric surgery can be risky and expensive, costing between twenty thousand and thirty-five thousand dollars, doctors are exploring alternatives such as medications that control appetite or restrict calorie absorption for obese children. However, most prescription and nonprescription weight-loss drugs have not been studied or approved for use in children or teens, so experts caution that young people should not take any medication for this purpose without being closely supervised by their doctor. Two drugs that have been approved for use in older children are sibutramine and orlistat.

Sibutramine

Sibutramine, marketed under the names Meridia and Reductil, is an appetite suppressant. It acts by increasing levels of serotonin and norepinephrine, which are chemical messengers in the brain. The increases fool the hypothalamus, a small section of the brain that regulates appetite, into believing more energy has been consumed than is actually the case, thus reducing appetite. Sibutramine has been linked to substantial increases in blood pressure and heart rate in some people, as well as seizures and bleeding. The U.S. Food and Drug Administration (FDA) has approved it for people who are sixteen years old and older. However, the FDA notes that sibutramine's effectiveness in treating pediatric obesity has not been studied adequately, and it therefore does not have enough data to recommend the drug's use in treating childhood obesity.

Orlistat

Orlistat is known as Xenical when obtained by prescription and as Alli when purchased over-the-counter. Approved for adolescents twelve years old and older, orlistat limits the amount of fat available to be absorbed by the digestive tract. When taken with meals, it binds with an enzyme called pancreatic lipase that the pancreas releases to break down fat molecules. As a result about one-third of the fats eaten are not broken down, and this undigested fat is expelled from the body without being absorbed. The fat soluble vitamins that are also excreted must be replaced by multivitamin supplements. Orlistat is intended to be part of a weight-loss program that includes a healthy, nutritious diet and

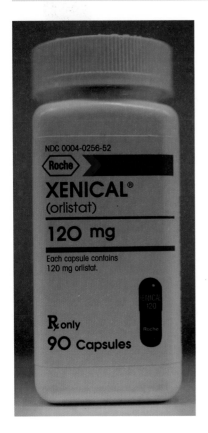

A bottle of Xenical, the brand-name prescription version of orlistat, is one of several drugs available to combat obesity. Orlistat, which limits the amount of fat absorbed by the body, is approved for use by adolescents as young as twelve, but it is known to have unpleasant side effects.

an exercise plan. However, in clinical trials, patients testing orlistat had a high dropout rate, stopping treatment due to unpleasant side effects such as cramping, diarrhea, and gas.

Little is known about the long-term effects of antiobesity medications on child growth and development. Critics note that children might get locked into lifelong use to prevent weight regain. This could be expensive, and it could be physically damaging if it is discovered that the drugs have dangerous side effects or are potentially addictive. Critics also fear medication might become the treatment of choice, seen by children, families, and doctors as a convenient quick fix for obesity, replacing safer, healthier alternatives like lifestyle modification.

CHAPTER FIVE

Living with Childhood Obesity

Youth who live with obesity face ongoing health, social, and psychological issues that do not affect most other young people. In countries such as the United States where being obese is viewed as unattractive, overweight children routinely deal with ridicule and rejection. One study that appeared in the *Journal of Personality and Social Psychology* in 1967 and is considered to be a classic in the field of social psychology showed that children as young as six years old described silhouettes of obese children as lazy, stupid, dirty, ugly, liars, and cheaters, indicating that obese kids are saddled with stereotypes early in life. Another important study done in 2003 at the University of California–San Diego compared obese children with those with normal body weights and to children with cancer and found that obesity had a physical, social, and emotional impact similar to cancer: "The quality of life for severely obese children and adolescents is roughly equivalent to that of pediatric cancer patients undergoing chemotherapy."[26] The obese children were socially isolated, missed school more often than other kids, and experienced ongoing physical distress.

One aspect of daily life that can be especially challenging for obese youth is managing the chronic health problems that often accompany obesity. Respiratory conditions, endocrine disorders, and severe pain are just some of the daily health issues that confront obese children and teens.

Living with Chronic Health Problems

Chronic diseases such as hybrid diabetes may force obese children to learn to incorporate daily treatments like self-injecting insulin to lower blood sugar into their lives. Like nonobese children with similar diseases, their conditions may prevent them from participating in activities with their peers, and they must come to terms at a young age with frightening potential out-

A boy with asthma uses an inhaler after exercising. Overweight children are often forced to make treatment for their resulting health conditions a part of their daily routines.

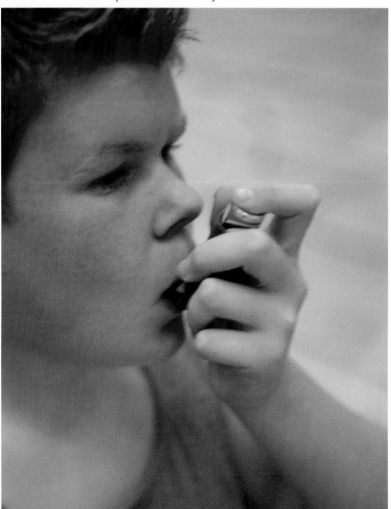

comes such as amputation or blindness in the case of diabetes, or gasping for breath in the case of asthma. While very young children cannot understand the risks and complications they may face, doctors generally advise parents to discuss such matters with kids who are old enough to comprehend the concepts of health and sickness. For example, doctors writing for the KidsHealth Web site about diabetes offer the following advice:

> Whether they're 7 or 17, kids think in the present, so you can't necessarily expect them to consider the long-term complications of diabetes as they go about their daily activities. When you're discussing long-term complications, it's a good idea to put them in the same context as you would when talking about health issues with a child without diabetes: Everyone needs to have healthy habits so we can live long, healthy lives.[27]

Orthopedic Conditions

Another chronic problem with which many obese youngsters contend is pain and subsequent difficulties in getting around. Bones and joints are not designed to carry excess amounts of weight, so obesity places unusual stress on these structures. Back pain, foot pain, hip pain, and osteoarthritis (the wearing down of the cartilage that protects the joints) commonly occur, limiting mobility. Not only does restricted movement impair a person's quality of life, but it can also prevent a person from exercising enough to lose weight.

Two common orthopedic complications of childhood obesity are slipped capital epiphysis and Blount's disease. "A slipped capital epiphysis occurs when two unfused portions on the neck of the femur [thigh bone or epiphysis] 'slip' apart, usually during the adolescent growth spurt. If not corrected, this condition can lead to permanent damage and a limping gait,"[28] explains an article in the *Osteopathic Family Physician News*. In Blount's disease, excess weight causes the tibia [shin bone] to bow, resulting in difficulty walking.

Respiratory and Sleep Disorders

Breathing is another area where obese youth face daily challenges. The respiratory system consists of the mouth, nose, trachea, lungs, and diaphragm. It supplies oxygen to the blood, which then delivers the oxygen to the entire body and removes carbon dioxide waste. Without oxygen, humans die. Obesity reduces the ability of the lungs to expand fully, so less oxygen gets delivered. Because of this, obese children are more likely to suffer from breathing difficulties than children of moderate weight.

When these breathing difficulties occur during sleep, it is often due to a condition called obstructive sleep apnea. This causes the individual to stop breathing and to wake up gasping for air. It results from the airway at the back of the throat being temporarily restricted, cutting off air to the lungs. Sleep apnea can affect nonobese people too, but it is more likely in those who are obese because fat deposits in the neck and throat can press on or block the airway. The lack of air causes oxygen deprivation, and the brain wakens the sleeper in response. After

A teenage girl uses an oxygen mask to treat sleep apnea, a dangerous, obesity-related condition that restricts airflow into the lungs.

the person takes in several deep breaths of air and falls asleep again, the cycle may be repeated numerous times. These disruptions interrupt the process of body maintenance and repair, and the loss of sleep leads to daytime drowsiness, which interferes with everyday functioning. In addition, loss of sleep has been found to coincide with increased appetite, because it increases a hunger hormone called ghrelin and decreases leptin, a hormone that triggers the sense of feeling full.

Endocrine Malfunction

Just as the respiratory system is impacted by obesity, so is the normal function of the endocrine system. The endocrine system consists of hormones and glands. Hormones are the chemical messengers that transmit information and instructions to various parts of the body. They are secreted by various organs, including glands, ready for transport to cells in other parts of the body. Together glands and hormones regulate such body functions as mood, growth, development, tissue function, metabolism, and sexual and reproductive processes.

Two examples of endocrine disruption in obese girls are early menstruation and polycystic ovary syndrome, also known as PCOS or Stein-Leventhal syndrome, which is a leading cause of infertility in women. PCOS is characterized by absent or irregular menstrual periods, an excess of male hormones leading to increased hairiness, acne, and weight gain, and is often accompanied by insulin resistance. In boys, endocrine malfunctions may result in early puberty and in an early end to skeletal growth.

Early Physical Maturation

The early physical maturation that may affect obese youth can lead to difficulties in their everyday lives. For example, adults may see them as older than they really are and have expectations of achievement and behavior the obese child is not yet ready to meet. A child may feel guilty for not being able to meet academic expectations or frustrated that he or she is never allowed simply to be a kid. Girls in particular may be targeted

Early Physical Maturation in Overweight Girls

Overweight girls seem to mature earlier, and this can lead to potential psychological problems for the girls. According to an article in *Time* magazine,

> It seems as if everywhere you turn these days—outside schools, on soccer fields, at the mall—there are more and more elementary schoolgirls whose bodies look like they belong in high school and more middle schoolers who look like college coeds. . . . Among Caucasian girls today, 1 in every 7 starts to develop breasts or pubic hair by age 8. Among African Americans, for reasons nobody quite understands, the figure is nearly 1 out of every 2. . . . Even more troubling than the physical changes is the potential psychological effect of premature sexual development on children who should be reading fairy tales, not fending off wolves. . . . The fear, among parents and professionals alike, is that young girls who look like teenagers will be under intense pressure to act like teenagers.

Although medical experts have proposed a variety of explanations for this trend, according to *Time*, "The theory that has the broadest support among scientists holds that early puberty is tied up with weight gain." Doctors suspect that the protein leptin, which is produced by fat cells, or high levels of insulin resulting from excess carbohydrate intake may be responsible for stimulating the early production of sex hormones.

Michael D. Lemonick, "Teens Before Their Time," *Time*, October 30, 2000. www.time.com/teach/psych/unit2_article6.html.

as their bodies mature, making them vulnerable to inappropriate sexual attention from older adolescents and adults, which they do not have the skills or confidence to deflect. Even if inappropriate sexual attention does not result in sexual contact, the implied expectations from the older person alone can trigger profound mistrust of others, leading to social isolation and impairing the child's ability to form future romantic relationships.

Psychosocial Consequences of Living with Childhood Obesity

The health consequences of obesity are just part of the challenges that obese children deal with on a daily basis. The stigmatization and discrimination they face can also damage the child's sense of well-being and ability to participate fully in the world around them. Health-care providers and parents usually focus on treating the medical aspects of childhood obesity, but children focus on the social consequences and perceive them as more serious. The 2003 University of California–San Diego study mentioned earlier also found that the psychosocial consequences of obesity, such as teasing and withdrawal from social situations, were more disturbing to the children than the physical distress stemming from their medical conditions. This led the researchers involved to recommend that parents and health professionals pay more attention to obese children's emotional and social needs.

The psychological stress that results from this constant harmful social bombardment from peers, teachers, parents, the public, and the media can trigger low self-esteem. This in turn affects academic performance, body image, and social interactions, and the negative consequences of these can last well into adulthood. A 1994 report by the National Education Association stated that "for fat students, the school experience is one of ongoing prejudice, unnoticed discrimination, and almost constant harassment. From nursery school through college, fat students experience ostracism, discouragement, and sometimes violence."[29]

A fourteen-year-old girl, who has decorated her bedroom with photos of pop star Britney Spears, looks in a mirror while holding her prom dress. Unrealistic media images as well as pressure from peers, parents, and others can affect the self-esteem and stress levels of obese teens.

One seventeen-year-old girl who weighed 440 pounds (200kg) wrote about how her obesity robbed her of a normal life: "I've been overweight since I was 12 years old. I used to go to school, but I had to drop out because people continued to make fun of me. I missed my whole teenage-hood because of my obesity."[30]

Discrimination and stigmatization can have educational, financial, as well as psychosocial consequences for obese children. They may be denied college placements in favor of thinner applicants with comparable test scores and grade point averages. This has been documented in studies such as "Obesity—Its Possible Effects on College Acceptance," reported by H. Canning and J. Mayer in the *New England Journal of Medicine*.

One widely publicized discrimination case that was eventually litigated in the U.S. Supreme Court in 1991 involved nursing student Sharon Russell, who weighed about 300 pounds (136kg). Russell sued Salve Regina College for intentional infliction of emotional distress, invasion of privacy, and nonperformance of its implied agreement to educate her after faculty and college officials harassed her about her obesity and dismissed her from the college when she would not lose weight. Russell completed her nursing degree at another school and won the lawsuit against Salve Regina.

Such discrimination may affect the future ability of obese youth to secure well-paying jobs as they move out of adolescence and into adulthood. Once out in the workforce, they can expect to face similar discrimination when it comes to promotion and pay. A 1993 study reported in the *New England Journal of Medicine* found that "overweight adolescents and young adults marry less often and have lower household incomes in early adult life than their nonoverweight counterparts, regardless of their socioeconomic origins and aptitude-test scores."[31]

Blaming the Victim

Much of the stigmatization and discrimination that obese children and teens experience results from commonly held opinions that being overweight is their own fault and therefore their own responsibility. Not only do many other children, teachers, and school administrators have preconceived notions about people who are obese, but studies have shown that even many health-care professionals hold these views. One study of over three hundred physicians found that two-thirds of them thought obese patients were lazy and lacked self-control. Another study found that over one-third of the physicians surveyed associated obesity with poor hygiene, hostility, and dishonesty. Other research has documented that many doctors and nurses prefer not to treat obese people because they believe these individuals are unwilling to follow treatment plans. Such attitudes may in turn lead obese people to hesitate to seek medical care, and even when they do seek care, medical offices and hospitals are not set up to handle their weight. For example, some obese adolescents are too big to fit into a hospital bed or onto the narrow platform on which they must lie to receive an MRI diagnostic test.

Obese youth must also contend with a world outside of school and medical settings that is built for thin people. Going through a subway turnstile or finding a seat on public transportation becomes a challenge. Even young children who are obese can have problems, as a man named Bo wrote: "As a young boy, I wanted to do the same things other boys did. I tried to ride bikes. But, my fat legs couldn't keep up. I sat in swings only to arise with chain marks on my legs. I remember not being able to fit into the school desk with the table top that you slide into. I had to sit at a table top desk with a free standing chair."[32]

Body Image

The difficulties in everyday life and cultural stereotypes that equate obesity with laziness and sloppiness can diminish an obese child's self-esteem to the point that they feel they are worthless. It takes a child of exceptionally strong character, with a very strong support system, to overcome the constant bombardment of negative messages that surround him or her. But many obese children lack such support, and even their parents may mock their weight. In her book *Fat Girl: A True Story*, Judith

A teenage girl discusses her obesity treatment with her doctor. Studies show that some physicians exhibit negative attitudes toward obese patients, who may then be reluctant to seek treatment.

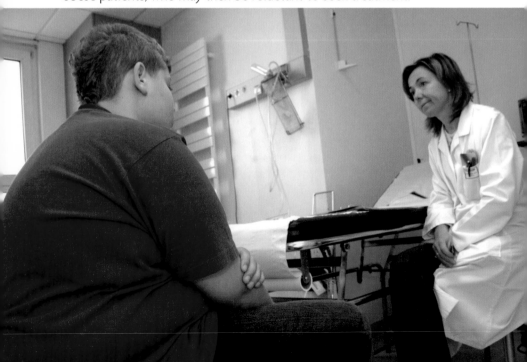

Eating for Comfort

While many obese children and adolescents become depressed because of their weight, the opposite is also true. Many overeat because they are already depressed, and they use food to comfort themselves. Maura, for example, tells her story:

> As far as I can remember, I began to overeat compulsively in seventh grade. It was a tough time for me (as it is for most girls)—physical development, social isolation, emotional imbalance. . . . I began to eat for comfort then, and gained weight as I was developing a woman's body. The taunts from my classmates at being slightly chubby led me to eat even more, and grow more and more fat . . . in eighth grade my self-loathing was increased a thousand-fold when I was sexually abused by my brother. And so the cycle increased—food comforted me.

> Once Maura realized that her overeating and obesity stemmed from her depression, she began getting help in the form of psychotherapy and antidepressant medication. When she started feeling better about herself, losing weight became a more viable possibility. "I'm really going to try to love myself, treat myself better. I hope losing weight will be a product of that," she says.

Quoted in Something Fishy Web site on Eating Disorders, "Personal Stories." www. something-fishy.org/whatarethey/coe_stories1.php.

Moore revealed that her mother taunted and beat her because of her fatness when she was a little girl. Moore wrote that as a child she wanted desperately to do the carefree things that nonobese children did with their parents, but it was not possible:

> What cut me deepest was when we went to the Macy's Thanksgiving Day Parade. What I saw there were little

girls riding on their father's shoulders; they had their hands around their father's necks and they threw back their heads and they wriggled and laughed. I would break a father's shoulders, I thought. I would break his neck. All his bones would crackle underneath my big hind end.[33]

Obese children and adolescents also take in the culture's obsessive idealization of thinness and may find themselves trying to resolve a negative body image through constant dieting for weight loss. The dieting may progress to become an eating disorder such as bulimia, where a large amount of food is consumed in a short time and then vomited immediately.

Some obese adolescents may smoke cigarettes, which contain the stimulant drug nicotine, to help them lose weight. This can increase their already higher-than-normal risk for cancer, heart disease, stroke, and death. Alcohol and other mood-altering chemical substances may also be used in an attempt to suppress the painful feelings arising out of low self-esteem. Alcohol increases the risk for diabetes, heart disease, and organ failure. Drugs such as marijuana can trigger underlying mental health problems such as psychotic disorder, an illness that disrupts the ability of the brain to distinguish between the real and the imaginary.

Anxiety and Depression

Given the physical and social stresses they endure, obese youth are particularly at risk for clinical disorders such as anxiety and depression. People experience anxiety when they find themselves in a situation in which they feel that they have no control and from which they feel they cannot escape. The resulting stress can trigger the physical symptoms that usually accompany fear, such as rapid heartbeat, nausea, and trembling. It can prompt the sufferer to avoid any situations (social events, sports, and so forth) that might lead to anxiety.

Depression is a condition that affects the mood and the body. Sleep, appetite, concentration, and energy can all be affected, and the person feels helpless, hopeless, and unable

Overweight children are susceptible to anxiety and depression as they struggle with the physical and social stresses of their condition.

to handle life's daily challenges. Children with a depressive illness cannot simply change their mood through willpower or positive thinking. If untreated, depressive symptoms can last for weeks, months, or years, and despair can become so acute that it may even lead to suicide. A 2003 study on weight-based teasing found that children who were teased about their weight were two to three times more likely to experience thoughts of killing themselves or to actually attempt suicide.

Addressing Psychosocial Factors

Given the enormous psychosocial burden carried by obese children, advocacy groups such as the Obesity Action Coalition and government health agencies have begun to address the psychological and social challenges that these individuals face. One way that advocates are trying to improve matters is through education to make parents, teachers, health-care professionals, and others aware of the need to treat obese children respectfully. In addition to promoting education programs, advocates encourage obese individuals to "communicate to the perpetrator of bias that his or her comments were inappropriate and hurtful, and that nobody deserves such unkind remarks, regardless of their weight."[34] As difficult as this may be, especially for young children, advocates believe that educating parents, teachers, and health-care professionals about the need to support obese children in their efforts to stand up for themselves can help a child gain the courage to do so.

Another way of addressing the psychosocial needs of obese children is through legislation that protects them from discrimination. Some states and localities, such as Michigan, Washington, D.C., and Santa Cruz, California, have already enacted laws protecting the obese, and others are considering such legislation as a result of efforts by advocacy groups. As Joseph Nadglowski Jr., president and CEO of the Obesity Action Coalition, stated, "Obesity carries with it one of the last forms of socially acceptable discrimination. We, as a society, need to make every possible effort to eradicate it from our culture."[35]

CHAPTER SIX

Looking to the Future

As the incidence of childhood obesity and its associated problems have skyrocketed worldwide, health experts such as Sonia Caprio of the Yale University School of Medicine note that "until recently, childhood obesity has been considered a clinical problem for specialist pediatricians. Now, however, the problem must be approached in a more global manner. The public health community must consider the urgent need to institute preventive programs."[36] Since policy makers are reluctant to introduce changes, especially if the changes are unpopular or expensive, it is important, Caprio explains, to prove that preventive or treatment programs would be helpful and effective.

National Response

In the United States, social policy and political decision makers are responding to medical experts' testimony that childhood obesity is endangering the health and longevity of millions of people and placing an increasingly heavy strain on the health-care system. National health organizations such as the National Institutes of Health (NIH) and the CDC are promoting research and prevention programs in an effort to reduce the incidence and devastating effects of the childhood obesity epidemic in the future.

The NIH funds more than 90 percent of all obesity research in the United States. In 2004 the NIH published the Strategic Plan for NIH Obesity Research describing the research areas

A mother and daughter read through a booklet promoting good nutrition provided by a local social service agency. Community health organizations on local and national levels have implemented a range of programs and interventions to combat childhood obesity.

it supports and identifying the research areas most likely to result in effective solutions for the childhood obesity crisis. The Strategic Plan for NIH Obesity Research identifies four major research areas: (1) preventing and treating obesity through lifestyle modification; (2) preventing and treating obesity through medications, surgery, and other medical approaches; (3) breaking the link between obesity and its associated health conditions; and (4) crosscutting research that includes technology and development of research teams from multiple disciplines.

The first area of research, lifestyle modification, studies the effectiveness of specific dietary and activity changes, as well as further examining the impact of the environment, in altering childhood obesity. According to an article in the *Journal of Nutrition,* "The cornerstone of these preventive plans focuses on the need to promote lifelong healthy eating patterns with regular physical activity, thus maintaining a healthy weight throughout life."[37] Researchers are focusing on how best to encourage diet and exercise, family involvement, and education regarding healthy lifestyles.

Improving Access to Healthy Foods

To adopt healthy eating habits, children need access to affordable, healthy foods. One way of promoting this is for municipal governments to encourage supermarkets that carry such foods to locate in underserved areas. The NIH and other public

A school cafeteria serves fruit and vegetables to elementary students. Schools across the country are revising the types of foods offered in their lunch programs in order to promote nutrition and health among the children they serve.

health agencies have issued reports that document the effectiveness of various local programs directed at this problem.
Many cities have had success in providing financial incentives
to grocery stores that build in underserved areas where local
governments have helped finance rebuilding efforts to make
these areas more attractive. For example, in Newark, New Jersey, community groups offered tax breaks and other financial
incentives to developers to help them build a Pathmark Super-
market in an impoverished area of town, and the store later
reported being one of the most profitable in the chain. In other
places local planners and community groups are furnishing
smaller grocery stores with refrigerators to encourage them
to stock more fresh fruits and vegetables and are sponsoring
farmers' markets in underserved neighborhoods. In Oakland,
California, the California Food Policy Advocates worked with
owners of convenience markets to help raise funds so they
could stock and display more fresh produce. At the same time,
the group arranged for children to take field trips to these markets to learn about buying healthy foods.

In many localities officials are also implementing policies to
limit children's access to unhealthy foods in school. In 2005,
for example, California and New Jersey banned the sale of soft
drinks and junk food at public schools and ordered the schools
to replace these items with healthier choices like water, milk,
juice, yogurt, and fresh fruits and vegetables. Other states have
since adopted similar policies. Many school cafeterias have
replaced unhealthy foods like chips, french fries, hot dogs, and
packaged cakes with fresh deli sandwiches, salads, and pasta.
And many have found that children and teens have responded
enthusiastically to these changes. In one middle school in Ap-
tos, California, for instance, sales in the cafeteria and vending
machines increased after changes were implemented. In Des
Moines, Iowa, the food and nutrition director for the school
district reported that "students have learned the benefits of
eating fruits and vegetables and according to some parents,
have taken that knowledge home and have been eating healthier outside of school."[38]

The We Can! Initiative

Several National Institutes of Health agencies are working with schools and local and state governments to prevent childhood obesity. We Can! (Ways to Enhance Children's Activity and Nutrition) is one program that involves collaboration between the National Institute of Child Health and Human Development, the National Heart, Lung, and Blood Institute, the National Institute of Diabetes and Digestive and Kidney Diseases, and the National Cancer Institute. The goal of We Can! is to encourage family and community involvement in the fight against childhood obesity. The program provides research-based information and strategies to parents and caregivers to help them influence children to make improved food choices, do more exercise, and watch less television.

Restaurants in many places have responded to public concerns over nutrition by providing customers with information on the calories, fat, sodium, and sugar content of their menu items. McDonald's is one chain that provides such details. They have also added new salad, yogurt, fruit, and vegetable offerings to their menus to allow people to make healthier food choices.

Some legislators and public policy makers have even proposed taxing foods of low nutritional value in a manner similar to taxes on cigarettes to help cut down on the use of these foods. Such legislation was enacted in Great Britain, although it is controversial because many people do not like the idea of the government telling them what to eat. An article in *American* magazine pointed out some of the arguments against such taxes:

If the government insists on trying to reduce obesity, then a tax on fatty foods is not the way to do it. Proposed fat taxes target a list of foods, assigning a tax rate to every food product. Who is going to do this? Presumably, some government agency devoted to the nation's nutrition will declare which foods must be punished, then watch to see if they've driven down sales sufficiently.[39]

Increasing Physical Activity

In addition to efforts to improve access to healthy foods, government agencies and health-care experts have also emphasized the need to provide children with safe places to exercise, away from traffic and crime, and many localities are working to implement such improvements. In some communities, volunteers are reporting on specific street, sidewalk, and safety conditions that make walking and playing outdoors difficult or impossible, and city governments are using this information to develop plans to repave streets and sidewalks, build neighbor-

A physical education teacher leads first-graders in stretches during gym class at an elementary school. Efforts to improve children's health include expanding school physical education programs and changing school curriculums so that they promote a healthy lifestyle.

hood parks, and install lighting and security cameras to make these areas safer. Some communities are focusing on reducing crime through neighborhood watch programs and tougher criminal sentencing laws.

Other municipalities are implementing training programs that teach children about bicycle safety and the benefits of riding bicycles to school. For example, in Philadelphia, Pennsylvania, the school district and a local bicycle coalition developed a program to teach middle school students about bicycle safety and to promote cycling as part of a healthy lifestyle. Other cities are focusing on building safe and accessible bike paths and bike lanes on streets to encourage more bike riding.

Experts have also determined that children need access to quality physical education programs at school. "Physical education helps students develop the knowledge, attitudes, skills, behaviors, and confidence needed to be physically active for life, while providing an opportunity for students to be active during the school day,"[40] says the CDC. Currently, only Illinois requires daily physical education for students in grades kindergarten through 12, and even in that state many students are exempt if they substitute other activities or courses. The CDC and other public health agencies hope to increase the number of students participating and the number of schools requiring daily physical education by 2010. They have also recommended supplementary classroom instruction that teaches students the importance of leading active rather than sedentary lives, and they have emphasized that schools should encourage participation and enjoyment, rather than competition, in physical education classes.

Restricting Advertising of Unhealthy Foods

Efforts to make healthy dietary and activity changes in children's lives are also focusing on replacing junk food advertising with positive nutrition messages. According to a 2007 report on television advertising and children by the Kaiser Family Foundation, one out of every three ads targeted toward children is for food. Of these, 34 percent are for candy and snacks, 28 percent are for cereal, and 10 percent are for

Kraft Foods, maker of Oscar Mayer Lunchables, is one of many companies to voluntarily change its marketing strategies regarding food products aimed at children.

fast food. Zero ads are for fruits or vegetables. The report also cites the opinion of the Institute of Medicine, which reviewed research on food marketing and children's diets and concluded that "television advertising influences the food preferences, purchase requests, and diets, at least of children under age 12 years, and is associated with the increased rates of obesity among children and youth."[41]

Based on this evidence, the Institute of Medicine has recommended that advertisements on television, the Internet, and in grocery stores (where sugary or fatty foods are often placed at children's eye level) be limited through national legislation. Some health-care experts and lawmakers in the U.S. Congress have proposed giving the Federal Trade Commission the authority to regulate advertising directed at children under age eighteen. So far vigorous opposition, based on the contention that such laws would infringe on their right to free speech, by food and beverage companies and advertising agencies has prevented such legislation from being enacted. Some companies, however, such as Kraft Foods, Burger King, McDonald's, Coca-Cola, and General Mills, have voluntarily stopped marketing food of poor nutritional quality to children, and some have begun campaigns to actively encourage good health practices. McDonald's, for example, has launched a *Go Active with Ronald McDonald* show to promote physical activity and a Passport to Play program that encourages physical education teachers to teach games from around the world to add excitement to their classes.

Medications, Surgery, and Other Medical Approaches

While many preventive and treatment efforts are focused on promoting lifestyle changes, health experts also realize that the biological processes underlying obesity are important in addressing the obesity epidemic. The second primary area of research, medical approaches to conquering obesity, centers on understanding the biological processes that control appetite, energy use, and fat storage in the hope that such knowledge will lead to the development of new surgical procedures and medications to treat and prevent childhood obesity. Although changes in behavior and environment are the first choice for prevention and treatment, these changes are not always effective or practical in all cases. For example, obesity due to genetic abnormalities may not respond to such interventions and might require drug treatment.

Research on Genetic Factors

Researchers have shown that some individuals may inherit a tendency to become obese, but pinpointing which genes are involved and developing strategies to prevent and treat obesity through genetic manipulation are not easily achieved. Claude Bouchard is the director of the Pennington Biomedical Research Center at Louisiana State University in Baton Rouge and one of the foremost researchers on genetic influences on obesity. Bouchard explains that when scientists first began studying the connection between genes and obesity, they believed only a few genes were involved. However, he says, "it turns out this predisposition seems to be determined by a much larger number of genes and each seems to have only a small effect . . . we've probably looked at 50 different genes and we're still not able to draw an integrated picture of which genes are making a difference."[42]

People have about one hundred thousand genes, located on wormlike bodies called chromosomes, in the center, or nucleus, of each cell. Each gene gives the cell instructions for manufacturing and using various proteins that are necessary for body functions. Genetic abnormalities, or mutations, can

Studies involving rats have revealed information about genetic factors that affect obesity. Experiments have shown that mutations of the PMOC and LEP genes can result in obesity.

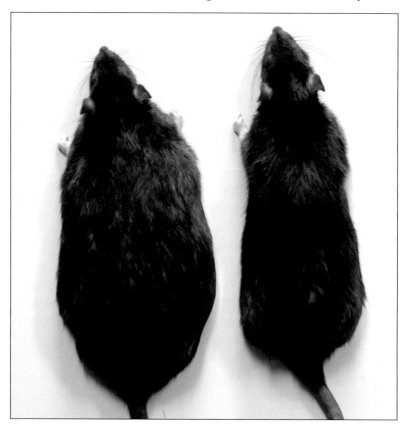

be passed to a child from either parent, since both contribute genetic material to their offspring. Scientists identify specific genes that may be involved in certain diseases and disorders by performing molecular genetic tests on tissue samples of people who suffer from these disorders.

One gene that scientists have linked to obesity is the pro-opiomelanocortin (POMC) gene. Researchers have determined that rats with a gene mutation that limits the production of the POMC protein quickly become obese. They believe POMC normally regulates appetite by acting on receptors in the hypothalamus area of the brain. Studies on POMC-deficient rats showed that administering a POMC protein called alpha-MSH led to a dramatic reduction in body weight, and scientists hope that similar interventions may prove helpful for obese people with similar gene mutations.

Another gene associated with obesity is the LEP gene, which codes for the protein leptin. Leptin plays a role in regulating thyroid hormone, a chemical that is critical for weight control, and in suppressing appetite. Doctors have found that people with a specific LEP mutation gain weight rapidly during infancy. Experiments where leptin-deficient children were given leptin injections resulted in appetite reduction and weight loss. However, this type of therapy may only be effective in people whose obesity is caused by an LEP mutation, and further research is needed to find out whether this is the case.

Biochemicals and Metabolic Pathways

Other efforts to understand the complex biological processes involved in appetite, energy use, and fat storage are focusing on determining exactly how the various body chemicals and pathways that regulate metabolism work. For instance, the NIH explains that "fundamental research on hormones produced by the gut, fat cells, and other organs and tissues is beginning to offer tantalizing hypotheses, at the molecular level, as to how the body's innate regulatory systems may make weight loss and maintenance of lost weight so challenging."[43] Researchers are therefore investigating various drugs that may target specific molecules or pathways. They are also examining the effects of children's age and stage of development on energy regulation in order to better adjust the timing of specific weight-control interventions.

One area of research on body chemicals that influence obesity has led to the discovery that the appetite-increasing hormone ghrelin, which is secreted by the stomach and the brain, is elevated in obese individuals following weight loss. This finding could help explain common difficulties in maintaining weight loss and may eventually be useful in developing effective drugs that target this problem. PYY3-36, another hormone produced in the gastrointestinal system, is also being studied as a potential basis for appetite-suppressing drugs. PYY3-36 is secreted after a person begins eating, and administering it as a drug may help reduce appetite and caloric intake.

Studies on the neurotransmitter dopamine have led to further possibilities for biochemical treatments for obesity. Dopamine plays a role in addiction to drugs, among other functions. One study found that obese people had reduced amounts of dopamine receptors in certain parts of their brains, and the higher the person's BMI, the fewer dopamine receptors they had. Similar deficiencies of dopamine receptors are seen in drug addicts, and researchers believe that dopamine deficiencies in some individuals may lead them to become addicted to eating too much as a way of compensating for this deficiency. Ultimately, such research could lead to new obesity treatments based on restoring dopamine.

Breaking the Link

The third major area of obesity research, breaking the link between obesity and associated health conditions, is exploring methods of preventing or delaying the serious diseases that often accompany obesity. For example, the Diabetes Prevention Program study tested various lifestyle and medical interventions as a way of preventing type 2 diabetes in obese patients with a high risk for diabetes. The administration of the diabetes drug metformin reduced diabetes risk by 31 percent, and lifestyle modifications such as improving diet and exercise reduced the risk by 58 percent. Another study showed that reducing television watching and video game use led to a significant decrease in obese children's risk of developing type 2 diabetes.

Other studies have addressed other diseases such as heart disease. The Cardiovascular Health in Children and Youth Study, for example, found that a combination of physical education and health education in schools led to greater improvements in children's cholesterol levels, blood pressure, body fat, and aerobic fitness than either approach alone. Another avenue of research centering on the relationship between visceral fat and metabolic syndrome found that mice that were genetically engineered to produce extra amounts of the enzyme 11beta HSD-1 developed both increased visceral fat and metabolic

How Scientists Identify Genes

Scientists identify specific genes that may contribute to certain diseases and disorders by performing molecular genetic tests on tissue samples from people who suffer from these disorders. One commonly used test is the Southern blot, named after Edwin Southern, the scientist who invented it in 1975. Researchers perform the Southern blot by placing a DNA sample on a special gel and separating the DNA by applying an electric current. The resulting DNA fragments are "blotted" onto a filter and identified using radioactive labels. This reveals whether or not a specific mutated gene is present.

Another widely used genetic test is called polymerase chain reaction (PCR). This technique was developed in 1985 by chemist Kary Mullis, who received a Nobel Prize for his work. Sometimes called DNA amplification, PCR involves separating and replicating DNA using temperature changes and a chemical called a polymerase. This allows scientists to fabricate billions of copies of a small piece of DNA in several hours and to analyze DNA pieces and locate gene mutations.

syndrome. Such studies may help investigators in their quest for treatments that can prevent both conditions.

Crosscutting Research

The fourth primary area of research, crosscutting research, combines several areas such as health disparities, technology, development of research teams from multiple disciplines, investigator training, translating research into interventions, and education. Ethnicity, income, literacy, and sex all affect access to health care. This means future diagnosis, prevention, and treatment options will depend on effective new research into these areas

A trainer for a mobile gym program in Miami, Florida, helps a boy with abdominal exercises. Some initiatives to combat obesity are especially targeted at poor and minority children, who often have limited access to health care and education.

and the sharing of information between researchers, health-care providers, policy makers, communities, parents, and children.

Data from the federal Agency for Healthcare Research and Quality reveals that poor and minority children have less access to and receive less preventive and ongoing care and education about conditions such as obesity. When they do receive care, it is less likely to involve follow-up measures. In response, initiatives such as Healthy People 2010 are promoting improvements in minority access to care by advocating public insurance coverage and issuing clinical guidelines to health-care providers that require certain standards of treatment for all patients.

Since only 22 percent of the medical schools in the United States offer required courses in nutrition, other crosscutting projects are funding programs that enhance nutrition education and emphasize prevention of obesity. These programs also seek to better educate medical professionals about the emotional traumas and health risks faced by obese individuals.

Other crosscutting research that NIH is promoting involves using biotechnology to support behavioral changes in preventing and treating obesity. Sensors and imaging devices that could accurately gauge energy intake and expenditure would be developed by biomedical engineers and obesity doctors to aid in the fight against obesity. For example, NIH is working with the U.S. Department of Energy to explore ways of producing oxygen-18, a form of oxygen that can be used to measure energy expenditure.

Looking Toward the Future

NIH and other public health agencies recognize that developing effective strategies for preventing and treating childhood obesity is a complex process that involves medical and behavioral experts, government, schools, community planners, and other disciplines. However, now that researchers are uncovering many of the relevant factors that combine to perpetuate this epidemic, these agencies are partnering with a variety of specialists to launch a well-coordinated effort toward addressing childhood obesity and its accompanying problems.

Notes

Introduction: A Preventable Public Health Problem

1. World Health Organization, "Childhood Overweight and Obesity." www.who.int/dietphysicalactivity/childhood/en/index.html.
2. World Health Organization, "Obesity and Overweight." www.who.int/mediacentre/factsheets/fs311/en/index.html.
3. Quoted in U.S. Department of Health and Human Services, "Overweight and Obesity Threaten U.S. Health Gains." www.surgeongeneral.gov/news/pressreleases/pr_obesity.htm.

Chapter One: What Is Childhood Obesity?

4. American Obesity Association, "Obesity Is a Chronic Disease." http://obesity.tempdomainname.com/treatment/obesity.shtml.
5. Quoted in About.com: Pediatrics, "Understanding BMI." http://pediatrics.about.com/od/bmi/a/06_bmi.htm.
6. Baylor College of Medicine, "Weigh BMI Limitations When Evaluating Children." www.kidsnutrition.org/consumer/nyc/volSU-ooe.htm.
7. Harvard Medical School, "Abdominal Fat and What to Do About It." www.health.harvard.edu/newsweek/Abdominal-fat-and-what-to-do-about-it.htm.

Chapter Two: Increased Health Risks of Childhood Obesity

8. KidsHealth, "High Blood Pressure Often Missed in Kids." http://kidshealth.org/research/hbp_kids.html.
9. The Mayo Clinic, "High Blood Pressure and Children: Watch Your Child's Weight." www.mayoclinic.com/health/high-blood-pressure/HI00049.
10. Quoted in Texas Children's Hospital, "Kids Courageous." www.texaschildrens.org/CareCenters/KidsCourageous/Gastro_Jennifer.aspx.

11. Quoted in Texas Children's Hospital, "Miracles in the Making." www.texaschildreshospital.org/Web/cmn/miracles/miracle_jennifer.htm.
12. *New England Journal of Medicine*, "A Potential Decline in Life Expectancy in the United States in the 21st Century." http://content.nejm.org/cgi/content/full/352/11/1138?ijkey=xvJS06bq8UHHc&keytype=ref&siteid=nejm.

Chapter Three: What Causes Childhood Obesity?

13. U.S. Department of Health and Human Services, *Dietary Guidelines for Americans, 2005*. www.health.gov/dietary guidelines/dga2005/document/pdf/DGA2005.pdf.
14. Hardin Memorial Hospital, "Weight Control and Diet." www.hmh.net/adam/patientreports/000053.htm.
15. Centers for Disease Control and Prevention, "Do Increased Portion Sizes Affect How Much We Eat?" www.cdc.gov/nccdphp/dnpa/nutrition/pdf/portion_size_research.pdf.
16. K.L. McConahay, H. Smiciklis-Wright, L.L. Birch, D.C. Mitchell, and M.F. Picciano, "Food Portions Are Positively Related to Energy Intake and Body Weight in Early Childhood," *Journal of Pediatrics*, March 2002. www.ncbi/nlm.nih.gov/pubmed/11953733?dopt=Abstract.
17. *American Journal of Clinical Nutrition*, "The Influence of Food Portion Size and Energy Density on Energy Intake: Implications for Weight Management." www.ajcn.org/cgi/content/full/82/1/2365.

Chapter Four: Treatment

18. Centers for Disease Control and Prevention, "Nutrition and the Health of Young People." www.cdc.gov/healthy youth/nutrition/pdf/facts.
19. Sarah E. Barlow and William H. Dietz, "Obesity Evaluation and Treatment: Expert Committee Recommendations," *Pediatrics*, September 1998, p. e29.
20. Quoted in American Dietetic Association Foundation, "American Dietetic Foundation's New Family Nutrition and Physical Activity Survey Reveals Health and Lifestyle Issues Affecting America's Families," News Release, August 13, 2003. www.eatright.org/cps/rde/xchg/ada/hs.xs/3662_ENU_HTML.cfm.

21. R.E. Kavey, S.R. Daniels, R.M. Lauer, D.L. Atkins, L.L. Hayman, and K. Taubert, "American Heart Association Guidelines for Primary Prevention of Atherosclerotic Cardiovascular Disease Beginning in Childhood," *Circulation*, 2003, pp. 1562–66

22. American Dietetic Association Foundation, "American Dietetic Association Foundation's New Family Nutrition and Physical Activity Survey Reveals Health and Lifestyle Issues Affecting America's Families."

23. Quoted in World Health Organization, "Malri's Story: Facing Obesity." www.who.int/features/2005/chronic_diseases/en/index.html.

24. Sonia Caprio, "Treating Child Obesity and Associated Medical Conditions," *Future of Children*, Spring 2006. www.futureofchildren.org/usr_doc/obesity_Volume_16,_Number_1_Spring_2006.pdf.

25. Duke University Weight Loss Surgery Center, "Understanding Obesity." http://secure.visualzen.com/duke/wlsc/understandingobesity/default.aspx.

Chapter Five: Living with Childhood Obesity

26. Jeffrey B. Schwimmer, Tasha M. Burwinkle, and James W. Varni, "Health-Related Quality of Life of Severely Obese Children and Adolescents," *Journal of the American Medical Association*, 2003, pp. 1813–19.

27. KidsHealth, "Long-Term Complications of Diabetes." www.kidshealth.org/parent/diabetes_basics/what/complication.html.

28. Rebecca Fahlgren, "Looking at Childhood Obesity," *Osteopathic Family Physician News*, July 7, 2007. www.acofp.org/publications/archives/0707/0707_1.html.

29. Quoted in Rebecca Puhl and Kelly D. Brownell, "Bias, Discrimination, and Obesity," *Obesity Outreach*, December 9, 2001, pp. 788–805.

30. Quoted in American Obesity Association, "My Story." http://obesity1.tempdomainname.com/subs/story/entirestory.shtml.

31. Steven L. Gortmaker, Aviva Must, James M. Perrin, Arthur M. Sobol, and William H. Dietz, "Social and Economic Consequences of Overweight in Adolescence and Young Adulthood," *New England Journal of Medicine*, pp. 1008–12.

32. Quoted in Obesity Help, "Bo's Journey." www.obesity help.com/member/72inches.
33. Quoted in National Public Radio, "From 'Fat Girl: A True Story.'" www.npr.org/templates/story/story .php?Id=4711959.
34. Rebecca Puhl, "Understanding the Negative Stigma of Obesity and Its Consequences," Obesity Action Coalition. www.obesityaction.org/resources/oacnews/oacnews3/ healthquanda2.php.
35. Quoted in Rudd Center for Food Policy and Obesity, Yale Univeristy, "Weight Bias: The Need for Public Policy," Obesity Action Coalition. www.obesityaction.org/about obesity/obesity/WeightBiasPolicyRuddReport.pdf.

Chapter Six: Looking to the Future

36. Caprio, "Treating Child Obesity and Associated Medical Conditions."
37. Tim Byers and Rebecca L. Sedjo, "Public Health Response to the Obesity Epidemic: Too Soon or Too Late?" *Journal of Nutrition*, February 2007, pp. 488–92.
38. Quoted in Joseph S. Enoch, "Senate Eyes Stricter School Lunch Standards," Consumer Affairs.com. www.consumer affairs.com/news04/2007/04/senate_school_lunch.html.
39. Adam Creighton, "Taxing Obesity: A Modest Proposal," *American*, August 2007. www.american.com/archive/ 2007/august_0807/taxing-obesity-a-modest-proposal.
40. Centers for Disease Control and Prevention, "Healthy Youth! Promoting Better Health Strategies." www.cdc.gov/Healthy Youth/physicalactivity/promoting_health/strategies/school.htm.
41. Quoted in Walter Gantz, Nancy Schwartz, James R. Angelini, and Victoria Rideout, "Food for Thought: Television and Food Advertising to Children in the United States," Henry J. Kaiser Family Foundation, March 28, 2007. www.kff.org/entmedia/upload/7618.pdf.
42. Quoted in Essential Science Indicators: Special Topics, "Obesity: An Interview with Dr. Claude Bouchard," March 2002. www.esi-topics.com/obesity/interviews/ClaudeBouchard.html.
43. National Institutes of Health, "Preventing and Treating Obesity Through Pharmacologic, Surgical, or Other Medical Approaches." www.obesityresearch.nih.gov/About/ Obesity_EntireDocument.pdf.

Glossary

autoimmune: A process in which the body's immune system mistakes normal body tissue for a foreign intruder and attacks it.

behavioral: Relating to a person's actions or reactions when facing situations or events; for example, overeating when anxious or depressed.

blood clot: Jellylike tissue formed by proteins in the blood to stop blood flow from an injury. Clots can form inside an artery that has walls damaged by plaque buildup. Clots that block an artery can cause heart attack or stroke.

blood pressure: The pressure of blood in the arteries as it is pumped by the heart.

chronic: Long-lasting and worsening gradually over time.

diagnosis: The process of identifying a medical condition or disease by its signs and symptoms and from the results of diagnostic tests.

dietitian: A health-care professional who specializes in food and nutrition, including weight control, healthy eating, and dietary management of diseases such as diabetes and cancer.

heredity: The passing of a genetic quality or trait from parent to child.

over-the-counter: Available for sale without a doctor's prescription.

sedentary: Doing much sitting; not physically active.

symptom: A physical condition that indicates the presence of a disease or disorder; for example, itchy skin and having sores that are slow to heal can be symptoms of type 2 diabetes.

Organizations to Contact

American Diabetes Association

National Call Center
1701 N. Beauregard St.
Alexandria, VA 22311
(800) DIABETES or (800) 342-2383
e-mail: AskADA@diabetes.org
www.diabetes.org

This Web site provides diabetes research information and advocacy.

American Dietetic Association

120 S. Riverside Plaza, Ste. 2000
Chicago, IL 60606
(800) 877-1600
www.eatright.org

This Web site provides food and nutrition guidelines for healthy living.

American Heart Association

National Center
7272 Greenville Ave.
Dallas, TX 75231
(800) AHA-USA-1 or (800) 242-8721
www.americanheart.org

The American Heart Association works to reduce cardiovascular disease and stroke.

American Obesity Association

1250 Twenty-fourth St. NW, Ste. 300
Washington, DC 20037

(202) 776-7711

www.obesity1.tempdomainname.com

This Web site provides comprehensive information on all aspects of obesity.

Centers for Disease Control and Prevention (CDC)

1600 Clifton Rd.

Atlanta, GA 30333

(404) 498-1515 or (800) 311-3435

www.cdc.gov

The CDC monitors public health, administers preventive programs, and provides public information.

National Center on Physical Activity and Disability

1640 W. Roosevelt Rd.

Chicago, IL 60608

(800) 900-8086

e-mail: ncpad@uic.edu

www.ncpad.org

The National Center on Physical Activity and Disability promotes the health benefits of physical activity and offers information and resources for people with disabilities.

National Institutes of Health (NIH)

9000 Rockville Pike

Bethesda, MD 20892

(301) 496-4000

www.nih.gov

The NIH is the primary federal agency that conducts and reports biomedical research.

The Obesity Society

8630 Fenton St., Ste. 918

Silver Spring, MD 20910

(301) 563-6526

www.obesity.org

The Obesity Society researches obesity causes and treatment.

World Health Organization (WHO)

Avenue Appia 20

CH-1211 Geneva 27

Switzerland

+41 22 791 2111

www.who.int

WHO is the international public health sector of the United Nations. It monitors and provides information on public health topics.

For Further Reading

Books

Eric Schlosser, *Fast Food Nation: The Dark Side of the All-American Meal*. New York: Houghton Mifflin, 2001. Provides a survey of the fast-food industry and its impact worldwide.

Brian Wansink, *Mindless Eating: Why We Eat More than We Think*. New York: Bantam, 2006. Examines the hidden cues that influence food choices and suggests ways to eat more mindfully and healthily.

Web Sites

Action for Healthy Kids (www.actionforhealthykids.org). Action for Healthy Kids is a nationwide, nonprofit organization that addresses the epidemic of overweight, undernourished, and sedentary youth by focusing on changes in schools.

Fruits and Veggies Matter (www.fruitsandveggiesmatter.gov). This Web site, provided by the Centers for Disease Control and Prevention, promotes fruits and vegetables for improved health.

How to Understand and Use the Nutrition Facts Label (www.cfsan.fda.gov/~dms/foodlab.html). This is the Web site of the U.S. Food and Drug Administration's Center for Food Safety and Applied Nutrition.

MyPyramid.gov (www.mypyramid.gov/kids/index.html). This Web site of the U.S. Department of Agriculture offers nutrition activities for children and tips for parents.

The Nutrition Source (www.hsph.harvard.edu/nutritionsource). This Web site of the Department of Nutrition at the Harvard School of Public Health offers information on healthy eating.

SmallStep Kids (www.smallstep.gov/kids/html/index.html). This Web site of the U.S. Department of Health and Human Services offers nutritional advice, games, and activities for children.

VERB: It's What You Do (www.verbnow.com). VERB: It's What You Do is a campaign by the Centers for Disease Control and Prevention and the National Institutes of Health to increase physical activity in children.

Index

Picture Credits

Cover photo: © Mark Richards/Corbis
AJPhoto/Hôpital Américain/Photo Researchers, Inc., 34
AJPhoto/Hôpital de Pédiatrie et de Rééducation de Bullion/
    Photo Researchers, Inc., 76
Altrendo Images/Getty Images, 53, 79
AP Images, 8, 14, 40, 43, 45, 47, 49, 61, 82, 83, 86
Jana Birchum/Getty Images, 38
Cengage Learning, Gale, 35, 54, 64
Mauro Fermariello/Photo Researchers, Inc., 22
Peter Gardiner/Photo Researchers, Inc., 25
Gusto/Photo Researchers, Inc., 30, 68
Image copyright Anita Patterson Peppers, 2008. Used under
    license from Shutterstock.com, 58
Image copyright Gordana Sermek, 2008. Used under license
    from Shutterstock.com, 56
© Karen Kasmauski/Corbis, 31, 70
Dorling Kindersley/Getty Images, 18
Living Art Enterprises, LLC/Photo Researchers, Inc., 21
Susumu Nishinaga/Photo Researchers, Inc., 11
Joe Raedle/Getty Images, 66, 88, 94
© Mark Richards/Corbis, 74
Thos Robinson/Getty Images, 41
Science Source/Photo Researchers, Inc., 27
© Visuals Unlimited/Corbis, 63
Voisin/Phanie/Photo Researchers, Inc., 90
Bobby Yip/Reuters/Landov, 28

About the Author

M.N. Jimerson has worked as a mental health crisis counselor and as a Web site manager for medical practices. She home-schools her teen daughter and is the author of another Lucent Books title, *Understanding* The Crucible. Jimerson lives in Massachusetts.